Don't Hug Me, I'm Pregnant

Book and Lyrics by
Phil Olson

Music by
Paul Olson

A SAMUEL FRENCH ACTING EDITION

SAMUEL FRENCH

FOUNDED 1830

SAMUELFRENCH.COM

ISBN 978-0-573-70023-1   Printed in U.S.A.   #28047

RENTAL MATERIALS

An orchestration consisting of **Vocal Score**, **Rehearsal CD**, and **Performance CD** will be loaned two months prior to the production ONLY on the receipt of the Licensing Fee quoted for all performances, the rental fee and a refundable deposit.

Please contact Samuel French for perusal of the music materials as well as a performance license application.

IMPORTANT BILLING AND CREDIT
REQUIREMENTS

All producers of *DON'T HUG ME, I'M PREGNANT must* give credit to the Authors of the Play in all programs distributed in connection with performances of the Play, and in all instances in which the title of the Play appears for the purposes of advertising, publicizing or otherwise exploiting the Play and/or a production. The names of the Authors *must* appear on a separate line on which no other name appears, immediately following the title and *must* appear in size of type not less than fifty percent of the size of the title type.

DON'T HUG ME I'M PREGNANT was first produced at The Secret Rose Theatre in Los Angeles, California, in September 2011. It was directed by Doug Engalla, the choreography was by Stan Mazin, the producer was DHM Productions, Inc., and the associate producers were Brenda Hensley and Laura Coker. The orchestrations and arrangements were by Paul Olson and Paul Moser, the set design and construction was by Chris Winfield, the lighting and sound design was by Mike Rademaekers, the stage manager was Liza Standish, the sound technician was Heliana Martinez, the publicist was Nora Feldman, and the cover art was by Cecily Willis. The cast, in order of appearance, was as follows:

GUNNER.. Patrick Foley
KANUTE .... Bert Emmett
CLARA.. Rebekah Dunn
BERNICE.. Natalie Lander
AARVID .... Greg Barnett

The understudy was Laurie Morgan (**CLARA**).

CHARACTERS

CLARA JOHNSON - Gunner's wife. Strong willed co-owner of a bar called The Bunyan, who's been married to Gunner for a long time. Clara is 8 1/2 months pregnant with their first child, very hormonal, but sympathetic.

GUNNER JOHNSON - Clara's husband. Strong willed co-owner of The Bunyan. A north woods Archie Bunker.

BERNICE LUNDSTROM - Pretty, young, wholesome, innocent, ex-waitress at The Bunyan. Dreams of going to Broadway.

KANUTE GUNDERSON - Oblivious, dense, harmless, full of himself business owner.

AARVID GISSELSEN - Slick, fast-talking karaoke salesman. A north woods "Music Man."

AUTHOR'S NOTES

I tend to follow the advice, "write what you know." *Don't Hug Me, I'm Pregnant* is my sixth play (fourth musical) that takes place in a small town in northern Minnesota. I grew up in a Scandinavian household just outside of the Twin Cities. My great grandparents on both sides of the family came over from Norway. On my dad's side they homesteaded a farm near Grand Forks, North Dakota. My mom's family ended up in Virginia, Minnesota, the iron range. My parents were actually related to each other before they were married which was somewhat disturbing to hear until I found out they were second cousins removed and not a blood relationship. Big sigh of relief.

Growing up in a Scandinavian household, I tend to write stories about the emotionally reserved nature of the people I grew up with. For instance, my play, *A Nice Family Gathering* (published by Samuel French), is a story about a man who loved his wife so much, he almost told her. I never actually heard my parents say they loved each other during the 44 years they were married. I'm sure they did love each other, they just didn't say it out loud. It was understood. And the closest we got to hugging was that awkward, arms straight out, patting each other on the shoulders kind of hug. We were strict observers of the "don't cross the bubble" rule. In the end my stories are about relationships, and how it's okay to say I love you or to hug someone. Enough said about that. The mushy talk is making me break out in a cold sweat.

Don't Hug Me, I'm Pregnant is the fourth in the *Don't Hug Me* series of musicals. The first three are *Don't Hug Me, A Don't Hug Me Christmas Carol*, and *A Don't Hug Me County Fair*. All four are stand alone musicals. You don't have to see them in any particular order to fully enjoy them. With that being said, I hope everyone sees all four of them.

Don't Hug Me, I'm Pregnant was booked into several theatres before I even finished writing it. Usually, you open in one city, play it for awhile, then if it has success you take it to another city, but because *Don't Hug Me, A Don't Hug Me Christmas Carol* and *A Don't Hug Me County Fair* have had such good success, theatres had a built in audience for *Don't Hug Me, I'm Pregnant*. And because the set is the same as the first three, and the cast is the same as the original, theatres that have done one of the others before have an easier time with casting and with the set. I'm fortunate to have Samuel French publish all four of them. They have been instrumental in the success of the *Don't Hug Me* musicals. They didn't pay me to say that.

The original *Don't Hug Me* opened in 2003 in Los Angeles where it won four Artistic Director Achievement Awards including Best Original Musical, and is currently playing in theatres all around the country.

The Christmas sequel, *A Don't Hug Me Christmas Carol*, opened in 2006 in Los Angeles, where it was awarded Best Musical of 2006 by Review-Plays.com. *A Don't Hug Me Christmas Carol* is a spoof of Charles Dickens'

A Christmas Carol, set in a little bar in northern Minnesota. What's really fun about spoofing *A Christmas Carol* is that most people know the story, and most of the story takes place in the dream sequence, the ghost of Christmas past, present and future. Anything can happen in a dream and it does in *A Don't Hug Me Christmas Carol,* with our Minnesota version of Scrooge, Tiny Tim and the Grim Reaper.

A Don't Hug Me County Fair opened in Los Angeles in February of 2009 to critical acclaim, winning four Artistic Director Achievement Awards including Best Author Original Musical. The story takes place during the county fair in Bunyan Bay, Minnesota. This year the Bunyan County Fair means one thing to Gunner and Clara Johnson, owners of a little bar called The Bunyan; The Miss Walleye Queen Competition. Bernice, the pretty waitress, sees this as her big chance to win Miss Walleye Queen, to be discovered, and to have her face carved in butter at the State Fair. The trouble begins when Gunner's wife, Clara, decides she also wants to win Miss Walleye Queen, and when Gunner's estranged twin sister, Trigger, shows up to try to win the beauty pageant, things get real ugly. One of the things I love about *A Don't Hug Me County Fair* is the fun beauty pageant on stage and that Gunner's twin sister, Trigger, is played by Gunner.

Don't Hug Me, I'm Pregnant opened in Los Angeles in September of 2011, to critical acclaim, once again set in Bunyan Bay, Minnesota, in a little north woods bar called "The Bunyan," owned by Clara and Gunner Johnson. Clara is 8 1/2 months pregnant with their first child, and today she's looking forward to her baby shower, getting lots of presents, and taking a break from her raging hormones. Suddenly, a freak snow storm, a "tsnownami," hits Bunyan Bay and they find themselves snowed in. No one can get in or leave. Gunner's worst nightmare comes true when Clara goes into labor and he realizes he's going to have to deliver the baby in the bar. So many people can relate to the whole pregnancy ordeal and have been very complimentary of *Don't Hug Me, I'm Pregnant* saying they think it's the best out of the four.

I wrote *Don't Hug Me, A Don't Hug Me Christmas Carol, A Don't Hug Me County Fair* and *Don't Hug Me, I'm Pregnant* with my brother, Paul. I wrote the book and lyrics and my brother wrote the music. Paul is a Nephrologist (kidneys) in Chaska, Minnesota, and I live in Los Angeles. Because of the distance, Paul writes the music first, then emails me a computer file of the lead sheets. I download the music file and write the lyrics to the music. Some people write the lyrics first, then the music. It works best for us to do it the other way.

Many thanks to Samuel French for all their support!

For more information about *Don't Hug Me, I'm Pregnant* and to see production photos, and song and video clips from the world premiere, please visit DontHugMe.com.

- Phil Olson
2012

SCENES AND MUSICAL NUMBERS

ACT ONE

Early October at The Bunyan, a little bar in a small northern Minnesota town called Bunyan Bay.

"Drinkin' Beer" . . . . GUNNER, KANUTE

"Don't Hug Me" . . . . CLARA

"If I Only Had a Boy" . . . . GUNNER

"Babies and Beer" . . . . .KANUTE

"I'm in Love With Another Man" . . . . BERNICE

"Marry Me" . . . . AARVID

"The 'Just Got Hosed Over by a Dork' Blues" . . . . .KANUTE

"Baby Fever" . . . . CLARA

"Lady Place" . . . . .GUNNER, AARVID, BERNICE, KANUTE

ACT TWO

One minute later.

"Knee Deep" . . . . BERNICE

"Stuck in a Snow Storm" . . . . .KANUTE

"If Men Had Babies, We'd All Be Extinct" . . . . CLARA, GUNNER

"When You Have Babies" . . . . AARVID

"Little Miss Muffet" . . . . BERNICE

"Bun in the Oven" . . . . . . CLARA, BERNICE, GUNNER, AARVID, KANUTE

"Relax the Nerves" . . . . AARVID, KANUTE, BERNICE

"Words Can't Express" . . . . GUNNER

"Babies and Beer - Reprise" . . . . .ENSEMBLE

ACT 1

SCENE 1

(The play takes place in Bunyan Bay, a small town in northern Minnesota. The set is a local bar, "The Bunyan," complete with stuffed fish, deer heads, and Leinenkugel, Grain Belt, and Schlitz Beer signs on the walls. There's a small bar, stage right, with two bar stools, a table, center stage, and another table, stage left, with two chairs at each table. Behind the bar are liquor bottles and sports trophies.)

(On the bar is a telephone, a radio, a bowl of beer nuts, a jar of beef jerky, and a small video camera. In the corner, far stage left, is a large karaoke machine. The front door is up stage, center. Next to the door is a window.)

(The music starts. Lights up on GUNNER and KANUTE playing cards, with two empty beer mugs in front of them. GUNNER is behind the bar, KANUTE is sitting on a bar stool in front of the bar.)

SONG - "Drinkin' Beer"

GUNNER & KANUTE. *(singing)*
DOIN' NOTHIN' SITTIN' HERE.
PLAYIN' CARDS AND DRINKIN' BEER.
MANLY MEN WITH AFTER SHAVE.
IN OUR NORTH WOODS MAN CAVE.

(GUNNER discards.)

KANUTE.
THAT MOVE'S A MIGHTY BOLD ONE.
GUNNER.
I PLAY WITHOUT A CARE.

9

KANUTE. *(holding up his empty beer mug)*
    HOW 'BOUT ANOTHER COLD ONE.

    *(GUNNER reaches under the bar and brings up two more
    beer mugs, 3/4 full of beer. He hands one to KANUTE.)*

GUNNER & KANUTE.
    IT MUST BE NOON SOMEWHERE.

    (They click beer mugs.)

    GOT NO WORRIES GOT NO STRIFE.
    GOT A PERFECT MAN CAVE LIFE.
    NOTHIN' COULD GO WRONG TODAY,
    RIGHT HERE IN BUNYAN BAY.
    NOTHIN' COULD COME THRU THAT DOOR,

    (They both point to the door.)

    THE DOOR THAT WE ARE POINTING TO,
    NOTHIN' COULD COME THRU THAT DOOR
    TO DISRUPT THIS GREAT DAY.

    *(CLARA enters the bar carrying a bag of groceries in each
    arm. She shuts the door behind her and leans against
    the door, out of breath. She's 8 1/2 months pregnant,
    very uncomfortable, looking like she's about to pop at
    any time.)*

    *(GUNNER and KANUTE are entrenched in their card
    game, not noticing CLARA. GUNNER discards. KANUTE
    picks it up.)*

CLARA. *(catching her breath)* Oh, for cryin' out loud, it's
    snowin' out there. It's barely October.

KANUTE. *(laying his cards down)* Gin.

GUNNER. Oh, for Pete's sake.

    (GUNNER throws his cards down.)

CLARA. Hey, guys, can I get a little help over here?

GUNNER. *(not hearing CLARA)* One more game.

KANUTE. You said that last time.

GUNNER. Just deal.

    (KANUTE gathers the cards to shuffle and deal them.)

CLARA. I mean, I hate to break up your 11 a.m. beer drinkin' card game, but I am eight and a half months pregnant–

KANUTE. Oh, I hear it's supposed to snow today.

GUNNER. *(watching* KANUTE *shuffle and deal)* Yah, I heard–

CLARA. Oh, for spittin' in the laundry, can I get a hand, here?

*(*GUNNER *finally looks up and sees* CLARA. *Thinking it might be funny,* GUNNER *and* KANUTE *both applaud.)*

(incredulous) Oh, no, you did <u>NOT</u> just do that!

KANUTE. *(to* GUNNER*)* Run. Just run. Go out the window. I'll distract her.

*(*KANUTE *picks up the video camera from the bar and starts to film* CLARA *and* GUNNER.*)*

GUNNER. *(walking over to* CLARA*)* Oh, c'mon, Clara, we were just kiddin' around, okay?

(He takes the groceries from her and goes into the kitchen. CLARA *goes behind the bar, takes a bite of beef jerky, and wipes down the bar with a towel.)*

CLARA. *(gets emotional)* Eight and a half months pregnant, and no one cares about me.

(sees KANUTE *filming her)*

Turn that thing off.

KANUTE. *(filming)* What are ya carryin' groceries for, anyhow?

CLARA. I'm tryin' to motivate the baby to leave. *(She puts her hands on her stomach. Uncomfortable.)* Oh, it's really kickin' today.

KANUTE. Ya want me to massage it? I got some carnuba wax. *(zooming in on her stomach with the camera)*

CLARA. No, thanks. Gimme that.

(She takes the camera from KANUTE *and puts it behind the bar.)*

GUNNER. *(coming out of the kitchen, to* KANUTE*)* She gets a little more emotional every day–

CLARA. *(from behind the bar)* I AM NOT EMOTIONAL!–

GUNNER. Okay.

CLARA. *(feeling something, anxious)* Uh oh, my water just broke!

GUNNER. *(panicking)* Nobody panic! Nobody panic! What do we do?! What do we do?!

CLARA. Oh, no, I just peed a little. I'm okay…Gunner will you run to Harold's and buy me some panty liners?

GUNNER. Oh, you betcha, honey, just as soon as I blow my brains out.

CLARA. *(She grabs a towel and wipes down the center stage table. Emotional.)* Ya know, ya think you'd wanna help out just a little bit, okay. I mean, people are gonna start showin' up for the baby shower and the place isn't even ready.

GUNNER. I was just gonna do that.

KANUTE. *(overly excited)* Hey, Bernice is comin', right?

CLARA. Yah, don't get your panties in a bunch.

KANUTE. Won't happen. I'm goin' commando.

CLARA. *(looks at* KANUTE*)* I'm gonna barf.

(She drops the towel on the table and runs into the bathroom.)

GUNNER. *(Crossing to the bathroom. He stops outside the bathroom door.)* Oh, c'mon, Clara, you know how I feel about goin' down to Harold's and askin' him for, ya know, lady stuff. Can't ya just use some paper towels and duct tape?

(We hear CLARA *barfing.)*

KANUTE. Oh, she got behind that one.

GUNNER. You okay there, honey?

CLARA. *(coming out of the bathroom)* Yah, I'm good. *(She quickly stops.)* There's more.

(She hurries back into the bathroom and wretches.)

GUNNER. I can't believe she's still barfin'. First it was that morning sickness, now every time she eats somethin' and the baby kicks, she pukes.

(**CLARA** *comes out of the bathroom and blows in* **GUNNER**'*s face.*)

Ohh! Beef jerky!

CLARA. *(emotional)* Just a little reminder what I've been goin' thru for the last eight and a half months.

KANUTE. *(to* **GUNNER***)* Hey, let's chug every time she says "eight and a half months."

CLARA. *(Calmly grabbing* **KANUTE**'*s shirt and pulling him close, face to face. He winces at her bad breath.*) Oh, I'm sorry, Kanute, is there somethin' ya wanted to say?

KANUTE. *(wincing)* Ya wanna Tic Tac?

CLARA. *(letting go)* You think I need a Tic Tac?

(She cries.)

GUNNER. *(jumping between* **CLARA** *and* **KANUTE***)* No, honey, ya don't need a Tic Tac.

(He shoots a look at **KANUTE**. **KANUTE** *nods to* **GUNNER**, *"Yes, she does."*)

Okay, alright, I'll go to Harold's and get your pan... pan...

(He can't say "panty".)

CLARA. Oh, forget it. How can I expect ya to run an errand for me? You wouldn't even defend me from Pastor Larsen.

GUNNER. I what?

CLARA. Last night in my dream, Pastor Larsen was hiring actors for the manger scene and he needed a *cow*... You told him, "Clara's available!"

(She cries.)

GUNNER. Now I'm responsible for what I do in your dreams?

CLARA. Why would ya be? You're not responsible for gettin' the place ready for the baby shower. *(emotional)* I just want nice things for the baby in a caring environment, and I'm married to a man who loved his wife so much, he almost told her.

(She laughs, then on a dime turns and cries.)

GUNNER. Oh, come on, I just told ya last Christmas.

CLARA. *(going to the karaoke machine)* Sometimes I think my only friend is our self-startin' karaoke machine. *(She caresses the machine.)* Just say a word from a song title and it starts to play, just like magic.

GUNNER. *(goes to hug her)* Come here, honey, give me a hu…

(He can't say "hug.")

CLARA. *(holding up her hand, stopping him)* Don't hug me.

(The music starts.)

Oh, hey, look at that. It knows me better than Gunner. *(to the karaoke machine, hugging it)* I love you, LSS 562.

GUNNER. It's just a machine, honey.

(GUNNER *goes to hug her and she holds her hand up, stopping him.)*

SONG - "Don't Hug Me"

CLARA. *(singing)*
DON'T HUG ME
DON'T TOUCH ME
DON'T EVEN COME CLOSE TO ME
THAT HUGGIN' MADE MY GUT EXPAND.

(GUNNER *tries to hug her again. She holds her hand up, stopping him.)*

OH, NO, DON'T HUG ME
DON'T TOUCH ME
DON'T EVEN COME CLOSE TO ME
UNTIL I BIRTH THIS BABY GRAND.

I GIVE YOU ONE THING, JUST ONE THING,
TO DO WE AGREED,
SET UP THE PARTY FOR OUR FRIENDS.
THEY'RE BRINGIN' PRESENTS, NEW PRESENTS,
FOR BABY AND ME,
MAYBE A BOX OF DEPENDS.

I'D LIKE A STROLLER, A CAR SEAT,
AND MAYBE A HIGH CHAIR,
ALL THE THINGS TO RAISE OUR BABY RIGHT.
IF I CAN HOLD IT TOGETHER FOR JUST A FEW HOURS
    MORE,
WE'LL MAKE IT THRU WITHOUT A FIGHT.

KANUTE. *(fat chance)* Hah.

(**CLARA** *shoots him a look.*)

CLARA.

I FEEL LIKE CRYIN'
THEN DYIN', THEN HAPPY AS HECK.
HORMONES GO LOW AND THEN THEY PEAK.
MY BACK IS ACHIN', IT'S BREAKIN',
I FEEL LIKE SHAMU.
I HAVEN'T POOPED FOR A WEEK!

KANUTE. Ya will when the baby comes out.

(**CLARA** *cries.* **GUNNER** *tries again to hug* **CLARA** *and she holds her hand up, stopping him.*)

CLARA.

OH, NO DON'T HUG ME,
DON'T TOUCH ME,
DON'T EVEN COME CLOSE TO ME
UNTIL I BIRTH THIS BABY,
TIL I BIRTH THIS BABY,
TIL I BIRTH THIS BABY GRAND.

(*The song ends.*)

I feel better. No, I don't.

(**CLARA** *runs into the bathroom.* **BERNICE** *enters the bar carrying a gift bag with a baby gift.*)

BERNICE. Oh, my gosh. It's really snowin' out there.

KANUTE. You're here!

GUNNER. Hey, Bernice.

BERNICE. Hey Gunner… *(less enthusiastic)* Kanute.

KANUTE. *(holding his arms open for a hug)* How was the tour?

BERNICE. *(She ignores the hug. Instead she fist pumps his palm.)* Oh, it was awesome. Last week I played the Corn Palace in South Dakota. I was the opening singer for a Teddy Roosevelt impersonator.

KANUTE. Sah-weet!

(**CLARA** *comes out of the bathroom.*)

CLARA. I thought I heard ya out here.

BERNICE. *(She hugs* **CLARA.***)* Oh, hey, Clara. Oh, my gosh, look at you. You're huge!

CLARA. *(cries)* I know.

BERNICE. No, I mean, ya look great.

CLARA. I do?

BERNICE. Yah. I love your shirt.

CLARA. It used to be a dress. *(cries)*

BERNICE. Happy baby shower!

(*She hands the gift to* **CLARA.**)

CLARA. *(overly excited)* Oh, my gosh, it's a present! The first one! Oh, thank you! Thank you!

(**CLARA** *puts the gift on the bar.*)

KANUTE. I got a present for Bernice in my pocket.

CLARA. *(to* **KANUTE***)* Cool it. *(to* **BERNICE***)* Okay, so, who did ya invite?

BERNICE. Ruth, Helen, Martha, Judy, Sarah, Aarvid and Trigger.

GUNNER. *(concerned)* Oh, no, Trigger?!…You invited my twin sister?

BERNICE. Yah.

CLARA. *(to* **GUNNER***)* Deal with it.

GUNNER. *(forcing a smile, holding up a beer mug)* It's official. We're havin' a baby.

(He takes a drink of beer.)

CLARA. *We're* havin' a baby?

GUNNER. We're not?

CLARA. Okay, just to clarify, *I'm* havin' a baby. *Gunner* is havin' a beer.

BERNICE. *(to CLARA)* Oh, your first child. How long have ya been married?

CLARA. Since Moses.

BERNICE. It's a miracle baby!

CLARA. No, it's Gunner's.

BERNICE. Oh.

KANUTE. If babies are such miracles, why would they have a multi-million dollar industry to prevent 'em?

(Everyone looks at him, incredulous.)

Just askin'.

BERNICE. So, when are ya due?

CLARA. Two weeks.

KANUTE. Are ya gonna get a c-suction?

CLARA. No, I'm gonna have it vagina-ly.

GUNNER. Whoa! Whoa! Hold on, there.

KANUTE. Did she just say–

GUNNER. "Vanilla." She said, "Vanilla." Just drop it.

CLARA. We only get one night in the hospital with our insurance plan, so I might have it induced.

BERNICE. One night?

CLARA. Yah, that's cause Gunner is the cheapest man in the world. He's actually in the Guinness Book of World Records under *(to GUNNER)* "Cheapest Man in the World."

GUNNER. Daniel Boone didn't have a hospital. His kid turned out okay.

BERNICE. Can I feel it?

CLARA. Sure.

(BERNICE *puts her hand on* CLARA*'s stomach.*)

BERNICE. Oh, my gosh! It's really movin'.

CLARA. Yah, I think it's playin' racquetball in there.

KANUTE. How do ya get a racket in there?

(*They all look at* KANUTE.)

I mean, I understand how ya get a ball got in there, but the whole racket?–

BERNICE. Kanute.

KANUTE. Can I feel it?

CLARA. No.

KANUTE. I'll give ya 50 bucks.

CLARA. Make it a thousand.

KANUTE. Under the shirt?

(CLARA *thinks for a beat, then agrees, nodding "yes," then moves to* KANUTE *who moves to* CLARA. GUNNER *cuts them off, jumping between them.*)

GUNNER. Okay…You're not touchin' my wife's… (*trying to think of the word*) Lady business.

CLARA. We could use the money to buy a crib.

GUNNER. We *have* a crib. The one I made.

CLARA. It has nails stickin' out of it.

GUNNER. What, do ya wanna baby it?

(BERNICE *tapes a couple balloons on the wall behind the bar.*)

CLARA. Yah, cause it's a BABY!…When are we gonna get a real crib?

GUNNER. When they're free.

BERNICE. (*knowing something*) Maybe you'll get one at the shower.

(BERNICE *tapes balloons on the wall, stage left of the front door and stage right of the front door, and on the karaoke machine.*)

CLARA. *(hopeful)* Ya think?

(**BERNICE** *gestures "maybe."*)

BERNICE. Do ya know what it is?

GUNNER. We're hopin' for a human.

CLARA. We want it to be a surprise.

BERNICE. Did ya have an ultra-sound?

CLARA. Yah, but we asked the doctor not to tell us.

GUNNER. I don't care what it is, okay, as long as it's a healthy baby boy.

CLARA. That joke never gets old.

(*The music starts.* **GUNNER** *and* **CLARA** *look at the karaoke machine.*)

KANUTE. *(looking at the karaoke machine)* Oh, hey, good choice.

CLARA. *(Looking at a song menu. To* **GUNNER.***)* Really? Ya had to go with 142?

GUNNER. Excuse me, I'll take it from here.

CLARA. *(sarcastic)* Oh, goody.

SONG - "*If I Only Had A Boy*"

GUNNER. *(singing)*
IF I ONLY HAD A BABY BOY,

KANUTE.
A BABY BOY.

GUNNER.
A LITTLE MANLY BUNDLE OF JOY,

KANUTE.
MANLY JOY.

GUNNER.
I WOULD GIVE HIM A POCKET KNIFE
RATHER THAN A GIRLY TOY.

KANUTE.
NO GIRLY TOY.

GUNNER. (*GUNNER and* **KANUTE** *mime fishing, hunting, etc*)
    I'LL TAKE HIM FISHIN' ALL THRU THE NIGHT,
    AND THEN WE'LL GO HUNTIN' AT MORNIN' LIGHT.
    NO GIRLY PILLOW FIGHT,
    IF I HAD A LITTLE BOY.

KANUTE.
    A LITTLE MANLY BOY.

GUNNER.
    WE'LL GO TO A FOOTBALL GAME.
    NEVER SOCCER 'CAUSE IT'S TOO LAME.

KANUTE.
    REAL LAME.

GUNNER.
    WE WILL GO SKI-DOIN', TOBACCO CHEWIN',
    GUNNER WILL BE HIS NAME.

    (**GUNNER** *and* **KANUTE** *high five.*)

CLARA. Wait, what?

GUNNER.
    WITH A GIRL THERE IS CONSTANT FEAR,

KANUTE.
    LOTSA FEAR.

GUNNER.
    SHE WILL NOT LIKE HUNTIN' DEER.

KANUTE.
    NO DEER.

GUNNER.
    THAT SHE'D RATHER DRINK MERLOT
    THAN TO DRINK A MANLY BEER.

KANUTE. (*miming drinking a beer*) Glug, Glug, Glug, Glug.

GUNNER.
    WHAT IF SHE WOULD RATHER BE AT THE MALLS
    THAN SPEND TIME WITH DADDY OUT TIPPIN' COWS.

KANUTE. Mooo.

GUNNER.
    NO TWEEZIN' HAIRY BROWS
    IF I HAD A LITTLE BOY.

KANUTE.

A LITTLE MANLY BOY.

GUNNER.

I'LL TEACH HIM HOW TO CHANGE A TIRE,

KANUTE. *(miming jacking up a car)* Reek, reek.

GUNNER.

HOW TO BUILD A BIG CAMP FIRE.

KANUTE. *(miming a camp fire)* Whoosh.

GUNNER.

WE WILL GO BOW HUNTIN', FOOTBALL PUNTIN',
A MAN, WOMEN WILL DESIRE.

(**KANUTE** *poses like a model.*)

IF I ONLY HAD A BABY BOY,

KANUTE.

A BABY BOY.

GUNNER.

A LITTLE MANLY BUNDLE OF JOY,

KANUTE.

MANLY JOY.

GUNNER.

I WOULD GIVE HIM A NEW CHAIN SAW,
RATHER THAN A GIRLY TOY.

KANUTE.

NO GIRLY TOY.

GUNNER

A BOY WOULD MAKE DADDY LIVE HAPPILY,
A BABY GIRL SCARES THE LIVING CRAP OUT OF ME.
WE'LL EXTEND MY FAMILY TREE,
IF I HAD A BOY.

KANUTE.

A LITTLE MANLY BOY.

(*The song ends.* **BERNICE** *sees that* **CLARA** *is not impressed.*)

BERNICE. Umm, I'm sure Gunner would be just as happy with a girl. Wouldn't ya?

(**GUNNER** *thinks.*)

BERNICE. Wouldn't ya?

(**GUNNER** *thinks.*)

CLARA. *(sarcastic)* Wow, I am so in love with you right now.

GUNNER. Really? 'Cause–

CLARA. Sarcasm!

KANUTE. Oh, snap.

CLARA. Gunner, we haven't decided on a name yet.

GUNNER. What's wrong with "Gunner?"

CLARA. What if it's a girl?

GUNNER. *(ignoring* **CLARA**, *to* **KANUTE***)* I'm gonna raise him to be just like me.

CLARA. Yah, that's somethin' else we need to talk about.

BERNICE. Do ya have any names picked out?

CLARA. We have a couple.

KANUTE. Kanute!–

CLARA. Is not one of 'em.

KANUTE. No? Okay, I got some other ones, here. *(He takes out a list.)* They're kind of alternative cause, ya know, that's what's in right now. Okay, stop me when ya hear a good one. *(He reads the list.)* I-baby…McRib… Kardashian–

CLARA. Okay, thank you, we'll keep those in mind.

KANUTE. So, does it have all its fingers and toes? 'Cause I hear the babies come out all weird when the mother is old.

GUNNER. Kanute. (**GUNNER** *shakes his head, "no".*)

CLARA. Yah, thanks. I know I'm gettin' up there, okay? Ya don't have to remind me.

KANUTE. Oh, Clara, stop, you're not gettin' up there.

CLARA. *(smiles)* Thanks.

KANUTE. You're already there.

CLARA. *(turning on a dime)* I will cut you!

GUNNER. *(to* **KANUTE***)* Really? Ya had to take it one more?

KANUTE. *(to* **CLARA***)* I hear they value older women in Puerto Rico. You should go there.

CLARA. Where's a knife?!

(She hurries into the kitchen.)

GUNNER. *(to* KANUTE*)* What did I just say? *(to* BERNICE*)* She's a little hormonal–

CLARA. *(coming out of the kitchen)* I'm what?!–

GUNNER. Not hormonal at all.

BERNICE. Clara, the baby is gonna be fine.

GUNNER. Yah, it'll be fine, honey. And thanks for comin', Bernice. I really appreciate you helpin' Clara with the baby shower.

BERNICE. Oh, are you kiddin'? This is gonna be fun. We're gonna play party games and drink Cosmopolitans, and–

GUNNER. Okie, dokie, then, alrighty, okay. So, I'll see ya in a few days, then?

(He gets up to leave.)

CLARA. Where are *you* goin'?

GUNNER. Duck hunting. Yah, Kanute and I are goin' up to his cabin and–

CLARA. You're not goin' anywhere, McRib Baby Kardashian.

GUNNER. Why? You don't need me at the party.

CLARA. Gunner, my cervix is ripe!

KANUTE. Did she just say–

GUNNER. *(to* KANUTE*)* Circus. She said circus. *(whispers to* CLARA*)* Do ya have to use the lady words?

CLARA. The baby could come when you're gone.

GUNNER. Well, can't ya hold off till I get back? Ya know, cross your legs and squeeze or somethin'.

CLARA. *(to* BERNICE*)* I think I'm gonna start speed dating.

KANUTE. Oh, hey, I'll go out with ya. I love pregnant ladies. Aaoooga! Aaoooga! *(to* GUNNER, *holding his hand up for a high five)* Who's with me?

*(*GUNNER *just stares at him.)*

BERNICE. He has no filter.

GUNNER. Oh, c'mon, Clara, what am I gonna do if ya have the baby, anyway? Pace around in the waiting room?

CLARA. You're not gonna be in the waiting room, doofus. You're gonna be in the delivery room with me.

KANUTE. Can I be in the delivery room?

CLARA. No.

GUNNER. What am I gonna do in the delivery room?

CLARA. You're supposed to coach me on breathin' and stuff.

GUNNER. Oh, for crikey sake, ya already know how to breath.

(CLARA *sighs.*)

See? Done. Mission accomplished.

BERNICE. *(to GUNNER)* Why don't ya wanna be in the delivery room?

GUNNER. I don't wanna talk about it.

CLARA. We went to a Lamaze class. They had a video of a baby bein' born.

GUNNER. Ya know what, they really don't wanna hear this.

KANUTE. Yah, I do.

BERNICE. Me too.

CLARA. What's the big deal? Gunner fainted.

KANUTE. You fainted?

GUNNER. I had low blood sugar that day, okay? I just needed a Kit Kat Bar. *(to CLARA, sarcastic)* Thank you. *(whispers to her)* "Sarcasm."

KANUTE. Holy shishkabob.

CLARA. Gunner, you're not gonna faint. Well, ya might faint, but it's a hospital, and they have people there for that.

KANUTE. It's nothin' to be ashamed of, Gunner. A lot of people faint. And those people are called "girls."

BERNICE. Kanute.

KANUTE. I'm not sayin' it's not manly to faint, okay, I'm just sayin' ya might wanna put on some lipstick when ya wave to the sailors during fleet week. *(He holds his hand up for a high five from* **GUNNER**, *re: his joke.)* Up top.

*(**GUNNER** glares at him. **KANUTE** brings his hand down.)*

CLARA. Gunner hasn't been back to Lamaze class since.

GUNNER. Look, all I want is a smooth delivery, okay, and that ain't gonna happen if I'm in the delivery room.

CLARA. You're gonna be in the delivery room or I'm sellin' my bar and movin' to Fridley.

GUNNER. It's our bar, honey. We own it together.

CLARA. Not after the divorce settles.

KANUTE. Hey, Clara, ya need to give us a signal when you're havin' the baby. Some sort of code word or phrase, like… *(He gets an idea, motions like he's delivering.)* "Show me the money!" No. "Say hello to my little friend!" No. "Release the Kraken!"

CLARA. I'll release *your* Kraken.

KANUTE. Just some advice, Gunner. When she's delivering, don't look down… *(motions to* **CLARA**'s *"lower area")* there.

BERNICE. Why not? Child birth is beautiful.

KANUTE. *(He holds up a mug of beer.)* Okay, let's say you're drinkin' a frosty mug of Hamms, the good stuff. All of a sudden, a slimy, under-developed baby head pops out of the beer… *(He holds the beer mug in front of his face, then lowers the mug, contorting his face, like his head is coming out of the beer, making baby sounds.)* You'll never wanna tread in those waters again.

CLARA. It's a moot point anyway. I mean, when ya get married, sex is like Bigfoot. Ya know it exists, but ya never see it.

(She laughs, then turns on a dime and starts to cry.)

BERNICE. So…how did ya ever get pregnant?

CLARA. Oh, I cashed in the sex coupons Gunner gives me for my birthday…I had a whole drawer full of 'em.

GUNNER. See if ya get anymore of those.

CLARA. *(feeling a sharp pain)* Ohh! It's happening! It's happening!

GUNNER. *(panicking)* What?! The baby?!

CLARA. *(feeling indigestion)* No. Beef jerky is comin' back.

GUNNER. Would ya please stop scarin' me.

CLARA. So, honey, since you're not goin' duck hunting, how would ya like to make me a banana, prune sandwich?

GUNNER. *(to himself, crossing to the kitchen)* Oh, man, this whole pregnancy deal is a real pain.

CLARA. I'm sorry, what?

GUNNER. *(turning back, busted)* Did I say that out loud?

CLARA. I'll tell ya what pain is. Havin' a baby! Just so ya know, it's kinda like passing a watermelon outta your butt.

KANUTE. Oh, I did that this mornin'.

BERNICE. How is it you're still single.

CLARA. I am so sorry this "pregnancy deal" is an inconvenience to you.

GUNNER. Oh, c'mon, Clara, I didn't mean it, okay. *(to KANUTE)* Help me out here, would ya?

KANUTE. You wanna beer, Clara?

CLARA. No, thanks.

KANUTE. Oh, c'mon, you're drinkin' for two, now.

CLARA. Babies and beer. Really? You think that's a good combo?

KANUTE. Absolutely. Hey, my mom drank during her entire pregnancy and look how I turned out.

CLARA. Case closed.

(The music starts.)

KANUTE. *(re: the music)* Looks like I'm up.

CLARA. No, please, seriously.

SONG - *"Babies And Beer"*

KANUTE. *(singing)*

PEANUTS AND PRETZELS AND BABIES AND BEER.
IT MAKES THE WORLD GO ROUND.
HAVING A BEER WILL BRING JUBILANT CHEER,
AND HELP YOU STAY UNWOUND.

MOMMY WOULD NURSE ME WHILE "HAVING HER ALE."
SAID IT WAS SMOOTH AS SILK.
I'M HERE TO TELL YA THAT NOTHIN' TASTES BETTER
THAN A MOUTH FULL OF BEER FLAVORED MILK.

BABIES AND BEER,
BABIES AND BEER,
MAKES EVERYTHING ALL RIGHT.
CRYING NO MORE, WITH EVERY POUR,
YOU'LL SLEEP RIGHT THRU THE NIGHT.

TEETHING WILL STOP,
WITH EVERY POP.
WILL NOT EFFECT GROWTH RATE.
GRAB A COLD BEER, MOM, AND GIVE ME A PULL.
I NURSED TILL I WAS EIGHT.

FOOTBALL AND HUNTING AND BABIES AND BEER.
IS WHAT IT'S ALL ABOUT.
BONDING WITH MOMMY WHILE HAVING SOME CHEER,
A FROSTY MUG OF STOUT.

DON'T HAVE A PROBLEM I TURNED OUT JUST FINE,

CLARA. Hah!

KANUTE.

DRINKING SINCE I WAS BORN.
HAVING A COLD ONE WHILE WATCHING THE GAME WHY
    IT'S
BETTER THAN INTERNET PORN.

(Busted, he looks at the others.)

That I've heard so much about.
BABIES AND BEER,
BABIES AND BEER.
A WALK DOWN NATURE'S TRAIL.
LIFE IS A DREAM WITH BEER ICE CREAM,
IT'S GERBER'S GOLDEN ALE.

KANUTE.
>RAISING A BREW,
>HAPPY FOR YOU,
>EMOTIONS RUNNING FREE.
>BEST PART ABOUT IT YOU'RE MAKING A BUDDY,
>A BEER DRINKIN' BUDDY FOR ME.
>I'M SO DARN HAPPY YOU'RE MAKING A BUDDY,
>A BEER DRINKIN' BUDDY FOR ME.

CLARA. *(to* **GUNNER***)* How do ya go about gettin' a restraining order?

BERNICE. Kanute, ya don't need beer to have a good time.

KANUTE. What?

BERNICE. You can have fun without beer.

KANUTE. I'm sorry, I'm not followin' ya.

BERNICE. Never mind.

KANUTE. This might be a good time to submit my application.

>*(He hands a piece of paper to* **GUNNER***.)*

GUNNER. What's this?

KANUTE. I would like to be the Godfather to your baby.

>**(CLARA** *clears her throat while uttering, "Huh uh".)*

>I have three references, my own transportation, and I can speak English semi-fluently.

>**(CLARA** *again clears her throat uttering, "No way".)*

GUNNER. Yah, Kanute, we're gonna think about that, okay?

KANUTE. Yah, sure. Let me know, though, cause I got other offers. Oh, and to show ya I'm sincere, I got a baby shower present for ya, Gunner.

>*(He hands* **GUNNER** *a book,* Pregnancy for Dummies.*)*

GUNNER. *Pregnancy for Dummies. (He shows the others the book.)*

CLARA. Oh, well, that's appropriate.

KANUTE. Better late than never.

GUNNER. Yah, I don't need a book, okay?

(He hands the book back to KANUTE. BERNICE *takes it from* KANUTE *to look thru it.)*

KANUTE. Oh, c'mon, Gunner, there's a lot of good advice in there. *(pointing to the book in* BERNICE*'s hand)*

GUNNER. Daniel Boone didn't have a book, okay. Daniel Boone figured it out by himself. And he didn't have electricity either, or running water.

CLARA. Daniel Boone didn't have a baby. His wife did.

GUNNER. *(thinks)* I knew there was a flaw in that argument.

KANUTE. Just browse through it.

GUNNER. No, thanks.

CLARA. He won't read the book cause he doesn't love me.

(She cries.)

GUNNER. That's not true. I l-l-l… *(He can't say "love".)* what you said.

CLARA. *(sarcastic)* Convincing.

BERNICE. *(reading the book)* It says here a lot of women gain even *more* weight *after* they have the baby.

CLARA. *(emotional, to* GUNNER*)* Do I look fat to you?

GUNNER. She's testin' me.

CLARA. Answer the question.

(He doesn't know how to answer the question. He looks to KANUTE *for help.)*

Don't look at Kanute. Look at me. Do I look fat to you?

GUNNER. *(thinks)* No?

CLARA. LIAR!…Of course I'm fat, I'm 8 1/2 months pregnant!

GUNNER. Okay, that was a trap-door question. There's no right answer to that one.

CLARA. What else are ya lyin' about?…Are you seein' another woman?

GUNNER. What? No.

CLARA. It's that Julie Stromberg, isn't it?

GUNNER. I don't even know who that is.

CLARA. She works in the meat department at the Super Value. I bet ya think about her all day, that young little hussy with those tight fitting stretch pants, and the hair net, and...and her name tag right there on her lady front all...pronounced. *(motions with her hands)* "Look at me. Look at my name tag, right here on my lady front. Would ya like some pork chops? Huh? Cause I got 'em right here!" *(She grabs her "lady front" and cries.)*

GUNNER. Okay, honey, maybe we should go take a nap.

CLARA. If I can't trust you, then how are we ever gonna make it?

(cries)

GUNNER. *(taking her into the kitchen)* Oh, we're gonna make it, honey. Everything will be fine.

BERNICE. *(reading the book)* It says here ya get mood swings when you're pregnant.

GUNNER. *(sarcastic)* Noooooo... *(He turns to* CLARA *while saying "no," sees she's glaring at him and quickly changes tone.)* ...way is that true!

CLARA. *(as they disappear into the kitchen)* I don't know who I am anymore.

(She cries.)

KANUTE. Women. Ya can't live with 'em, oh, beer nuts.

(He grabs some beer nuts.)

GUNNER. *(coming out of the kitchen)* She'll be okay. She just needs a little rest.

CLARA. *(coming out of the kitchen)* I am not my mother!

GUNNER. Okay, honey. Let's get some rest.

CLARA. I just wanna feel attractive.

GUNNER. Why?

CLARA. *(cries)* Ohh!

GUNNER. I mean, you're not goin' out or anything. Ya don't need to look attractive. Just stay the way ya are.

CLARA. *(cries)* Ohh!

KANUTE. Hey, this might be a good time to give Clara her present. *(He takes out a breast pump from behind the bar.)* It's a breast pump. Here, I'll show ya how it works. I'm just gonna need ya to flip out one of your thingies– *(He holds the breast pump toward* **CLARA.***)*

GUNNER. *(***GUNNER** *grabs the breast pump from* **KANUTE***)* Okay...Not gonna happen.

KANUTE. Oh, I have somethin' for Bernice, too.

(He takes out a ring box from his pocket.)

BERNICE. *(Sees the ring. Panicking.)* Oh gosh, oh gosh–

KANUTE. *(to* **GUNNER** *and* **CLARA***)* I've had this since the last time I proposed. *(He gets down on one knee, and holds the box out to* **BERNICE.***)* Okay, so, umm, Bernice, ya know how I feel about ya, right?...Well...will you–

BERNICE. *(before* **KANUTE** *can finish the sentence)* I have an announcement.

KANUTE. Well, umm, can it wait, ya know, till I ask ya–

BERNICE. I'm gettin' married.

KANUTE. To me?

BERNICE. What? No, to Aarvid.

KANUTE. To Aarvid?

CLARA. Congratulations. Hopefully you'll be happy.

(She shoots a look a **GUNNER.***)*

GUNNER. Ya look great, honey–

CLARA. Shut it!–

GUNNER. Okay.

KANUTE. *(getting up)* But he sells karaoke machines.

BERNICE. Lifestyle systems.

KANUTE. Bernice, I thought we could, ya know, maybe be a couple again. I mean, we were engaged once.

BERNICE. I know, Kanute. That was a dark time in my life.

KANUTE. Yah, but see, that's perfect, cause I've changed. I'm funny now. I've been writin' jokes. Here's one I'm workin' on. *(He takes out a note card and reads it.)* Knock, knock.

BERNICE. *(reluctantly)* Who's there?

KANUTE. Yah, that's all I got so far…It's a work in progress.

BERNICE. I'm sorry, Kanute. It's just that, I'm in love.

> *(The music starts.)*

> Oh, a love song.

KANUTE. *(hopeful)* A love song to me?

BERNICE. You're in it.

KANUTE. Sweet!

> ***SONG - "I'm in Love With Another Man"***

BERNICE. *(sings)*

> I AM IN LOVE WITH ANOTHER MAN.
> ANOTHER MAN WHO ISN'T YOU.

> *(to* **KANUTE***)*

KANUTE. That's harsh.

BERNICE.

> HE HAS GOOD LOOKS, WIT AND CHARM
> AND A FIVE YEAR PLAN.
> A MAN I'LL MARRY SOON,

> *(***KANUTE*** stands)*

> NOT YOU.

GUNNER. Ouch.

> *(***KANUTE*** sits back down.)*

BERNICE.

> WE'LL HAVE THE WEDDING AT TWO
> AT THE OLD V.F.W.
> AT THE RECEPTION WE WILL HAVE A TUB
> OF CHEESE FONDUE.

> OH, YES, I'M SO DARN IN LOVE WITH A HANDSOME MAN.

KANUTE. *I'm* handsome.

BERNICE.

> A HANDSOME MAN WHO ISN'T HERE.

KANUTE. Crap.

BERNICE.

> HE HAS A JOB, WORKERS' COMP, AND A MINI-VAN.
> WHAT'S MORE WE LIKE THE SAME DRAFT BEER.

KANUTE. Well, I'm *rich.*

BERNICE.

> WE'LL HONEYMOON IN BUNYAN BAY,
> DINE AT SWEDE LARSON'S PORK BUFFET,
> AND AT THE MOTEL WE'LL BE MAKIN' BABIES
> NIGHT AND DAY.

KANUTE. I'm right here, ya know.

BERNICE.

> I AM IN LOVE WITH ANOTHER MAN.
> ANOTHER MAN WHO IS,
> ANOTHER MAN WHO IS,

CLARA. Everyone!

BERNICE & CLARA & GUNNER.

> ANOTHER MAN WHO ISN'T YOU.

(Everyone points to **KANUTE.** *)*

KANUTE. I really wanted to like that song.

*(***AARVID** *enters the bar with a shoulder bag.* **BERNICE** *is standing between the front door and the karaoke machine.)*

AARVID. Hey, everyone.

BERNICE & CLARA & GUNNER. Hey, Aarvid. How's it goin'? Good to see ya. (*etc.*)

AARVID. Who ordered the snow, huh?

*(***CLARA** *looks out the window.)*

CLARA. Yah, it's really comin' down out there. How are the roads?

AARVID. Brutal.

CLARA. Oh, cripes.

GUNNER. Don't worry, honey. They'll be here.

*(***AARVID** *looks over and sees the karaoke machine.* **BERNICE** *thinks he's looking at her.)*

AARVID. There she is.

(He walks over to the karaoke machine with arms out.)

(*BERNICE thinks he's going to hug her. He walks right past her to the karaoke machine.*)

AARVID. The LSS 562. (*He pats the machine and goes into "sales" mode.*) Featuring 82 songs by folk legend, Sven Yorgensen.

BERNICE & CLARA. (*dreamy*) Sven Yorgensen.

AARVID. Complete with intuitive voice activation. Powered by love, or electrical outlet.

KANUTE. Does he ever stop sellin'?

AARVID. (*seeing KANUTE, with a hostile attitude*) Kanute.

KANUTE. (*equally hostile*) Karaoke guy.

AARVID. (*seeing CLARA*) Oh, hey, you're pregnant!

CLARA. What? (*She looks at her stomach.*) Whoa! Where'd that come from?

AARVID. Who's the father? (*He laughs.*) Just kiddin'.

(*He looks at CLARA for confirmation on whether it's GUNNER.*)

It's Gunner, right?

GUNNER. Funny.

AARVID. (*He takes out a gift bag from his shoulder bag and hands it to CLARA.*) Oh, here. It's for the baby.

CLARA. (*overly excited*) Oh, another present! Another present! Thank you! Thank you!

(*She puts it on the bar.*)

KANUTE. (*with an attitude*) So, how's the karaoke business.

AARVID. Actually I'm lookin' at another job opportunity right now.

KANUTE. Why? No money in karaoke machines?

AARVID. Lifestyle systems.

KANUTE. Karaoke machines.

AARVID. Lifestyle systems. Why Lifestyle? Cause this little baby will change your life forever.

(*He pats the machine.*)

CLARA. *(to* **GUNNER***)* It brought romance back into our lives, remember?

GUNNER. *(unenthusiastic)* Sure do... *(to himself)* Dammit.

BERNICE. Aarvid is like a love doctor.

AARVID. *(spoken, melodramatic)* All ya need is love...Love... Love is all ya need.

BERNICE. *(enamored)* Oh, that could be a song.

CLARA. Congratulations, Aarvid.

AARVID. For what?

CLARA. Bernice told us the good news.

AARVID. What good news?

CLARA. That you and Bernice are gettin' married.

AARVID. We are?

KANUTE. Hey-yo!

BERNICE. Yes, silly. You proposed to me. Remember?

AARVID. Well, yah, but that was a long time ago. You said you couldn't get engaged.

BERNICE. Well, I couldn't get engaged cause I had to go on tour and stuff. I'm done touring.

AARVID. I thought ya wanted to pursue a singin' career. Ya know, be on *American Idol* and then Broadway. In that order.

BERNICE. I tried out for *American Idol.* They went with a stripper from Duluth.

KANUTE. Was it Sharlene?

(Everyone looks at him. He's busted.)

Who I don't know...but I read about in *Stripper News...* that I don't subscribe to. This is entrapment!

BERNICE. I can be engaged now.

AARVID. Well, that's great.

KANUTE. *(to* **BERNICE***)* Wait, wait, so, Aarvid didn't know he was engaged?

BERNICE. Well, no, but–

KANUTE. *(to* **AARVID***)* So, you haven't proposed since she turned ya down?

AARVID. Well, no, but–

CLARA. Ya know, maybe I should go do somethin' in the kitchen. Gunner?

GUNNER. No way. I'm stayin' for this.

KANUTE. *(to* **AARVID***)* Well, it's not official till you officially propose. And if you don't have the ring, you're not officially engaged.

BERNICE. Ya still have the ring, don't ya?

*(**AARVID** doesn't say anything.)*

Ya don't have the ring? What did ya do with it?

*(**AARVID** doesn't say anything.)*

Ya pawned it?

GUNNER. He doesn't even have to talk. It's like they're already married.

CLARA. Don't judge me! *(She turns on a dime and gets very nice.)* Beer anyone?

KANUTE. It's like Dr. Jekyl and Mr. Rogers.

AARVID. *(to* **BERNICE***)* Well, ya said "no" to me and I needed the money.

BERNICE. Kanute, where's your engagement ring?

KANUTE. Right here.

(He holds out the ring box.)

BERNICE. Okay, good. Now give it to Aarvid, would ya?

KANUTE. Okay. *(He starts to hand it to* **AARVID***, then stops.)* Wait, what?

BERNICE. If ya give your engagement ring to Aarvid, he can use it to propose to me.

KANUTE. Seems like kind of a conflict of interest, don't it?

CLARA. Now, who said Kanute wasn't smart?

*(Everyone but **BERNICE** raises their hand. Even **KANUTE** raises his hand.)*

BERNICE. *(getting very close to* **KANUTE***, flirty)* You want me to be happy, don't ya?

KANUTE. *I* can make ya happy. C'mon, Bernice, I own six campin', canoein', fishin' stores.

AARVID. How did he ever get six stores?

CLARA. He inherited 'em.

KANUTE. *(He makes a "Wookie" sound.)* Aaaaaaaaa…That's six in Wookie… *(to* **BERNICE**, *bragging)* I'm takin' the Rosetta Stone.

BERNICE. *(to* **KANUTE***)* Please?

KANUTE. You're not gettin' my ring unless ya marry me.

CLARA. Here, use this cigar band.

> *(hands* **AARVID** *a cigar band)*

KANUTE. What are ya doin'?

CLARA. *(to* **AARVID***)* It's just temporary, till ya get a real one. A good one.

KANUTE. Ya know, if ya marry *me*, you'd have a good ring right now.

CLARA. *(making a "Wookie" sound)* Aaaaaaaaa…That's Wookie for "shut your pie hole."

AARVID. Okay, ya know what. I wanna propose, okay. Cause I'm still in love with Bernice. So, okay, here we go.

> *(***AARVID*** *gets down on one knee, nervous about proposing.)*

KANUTE. Okay, I didn't wanna have to resort to this, but rock, paper, scissors for Bernice.

> *(He holds out his fist to* **AARVID**. **AARVID** *holds his fist out to compete. They start to pump their fists.)*

BERNICE. *(stopping them)* Hellooo! *(to* **AARVID***)* What are ya doin'?

AARVID. Sorry, I got caught up in the competition.

KANUTE. Bernice is right, not manly enough. We'll wrestle for her.

> *(He gets down on his hands and knees in a high school wrestling position, with his butt toward* **AARVID**.*)*

C'mon, let's do it!

AARVID. I'm not gonna wrestle you, Kanute.

KANUTE. C'mon, be a man. *(He spanks his butt.)* Now, get on!

BERNICE. *(helping* **KANUTE** *up)* Kanute, I'll always be your friend, okay, but my heart belongs to Aarvid. Aarvid is the one I love, and Aarvid is the one I'm gonna marry.

(**KANUTE** *leans into* **BERNICE,** *closes his eyes and puckers his lips to kiss her on the lips. She leans away.)*

What are ya doin'?

KANUTE. I'm sorry, I totally misread that.

AARVID. *(He gets down on one knee.)* Bernice, will you marry me?

BERNICE. Oh, my gosh! Oh, my gosh! Oh, my gosh! *(thinks)* Okay, can we try it over here? *(taking him to another part of the bar)*

AARVID. I didn't do it right the first time?

BERNICE. No, it's just that the fung shway is better here. I'm sorry, it's just that I wanna remember this day for the rest of my life, okay?

AARVID. Okay. *(He points to the karaoke machine.)* Marry me.

(The music starts. **AARVID***'s hips start moving to the music, a la John Travolta in* Saturday Night Fever.*)*

BERNICE. Oh, my gosh! He's gonna sing!

AARVID. *(looking at his hips moving)* Oh, that is strangely involuntary.

SONG - "Marry Me"

(He sings.)

YOU'RE EVERYTHING I DREAM ABOUT
YOU MEAN THE WORLD TO ME.
I'LL LOVE YOU TILL THE END OF TIME
OR MORE I GUARANTEE.

YOU'RE SPECIAL AND I DON'T MEAN SPECIAL
LIKE MY UNCLE BILL.
YOU'RE SPECIAL LIKE A NEW GEORGE FORMAN GRILL.

BERNICE. *(flattered)* Ohh.

AARVID.

MARRY ME.
HAPPY AS A CLAM WE'LL BE.
ALL THE WORLD WILL SEE
OUR TRUE LOVE WE EVOKE.

MARRY ME.
LOVE WILL CONQUER ALL YOU'LL SEE.
YOU'LL FIND LOVE WITH ME.
EVEN THO I AM BROKE.

(**BERNICE** *reacts to "broke" and the other things she learns about* **AARVID**.)

I LOVE YOU MORE THAN EVER
THO I'M IN A LITTLE DROUGHT.
AND JUST BECAUSE I LOST MY JOB
AND WORKERS' COMP RAN OUT.
AND THO I SOLD MY MINI-VAN
AND NOW I RIDE THE BUS.
OUR LOVE WILL GROW AS LONG AS WE HAVE US.

MARRY ME.
YOU'RE THE ONLY ONE FOR ME.
WE CAN SAVE MONEY
WITH NO WEDDING VEIL.

MARRY ME.
WE'LL HAVE CHERRIES JUBILEE
AT THE DAIRY QUEEN,
IT'S ON SALE.

(**AARVID** *gets down on one knee.*)

MARRY ME.
RUN AWAY AND MARRY ME.
CAUSE IF WE ELOPE IT'S FREE.
MARRY ME.
PLEASE MARRY ME.
WON'T YOU MARRY ME.
DEAR LORD MARRY ME.
MARRY, MARRY, MARRY ME.

KANUTE. Stop begging!

AARVID.

PLEASE MARRY ME.

BERNICE. So…what happened to your five year plan?

AARVID. Oh, it's better. Now it's a ten year plan. And I'm right on track. You have a job, right?

BERNICE. Umm…

AARVID. That's okay. I'm thinkin' of startin' a Lifestyle System franchise. *(gesturing a billboard)* "Bringing love back to Bunyan Bay." *(to **BERNICE**)* I'm gonna trademark that. Make T-shirts.

KANUTE. Awesome proposal. *(to **BERNICE**)* He had me at "lost my job."

AARVID. Well?

BERNICE. Yah, umm…how did Gunner propose to *you*, Clara?

CLARA. Oh, yah, okay, umm…well, it was in the summer. Do ya remember what day it was, Gunner?

GUNNER. Umm, Tuesday.

CLARA. Oh, my gosh, it was Saturday, July 8th. Ya don't even remember?

GUNNER. If ya knew, why did ya ask me?

CLARA. To see if ya love me.

GUNNER. Is this another test? 'Cause maybe I should just go study.

CLARA. It was July 8th. The sun was setting and Gunner asked me to go canoeing with him. Do you remember that part?

GUNNER. Yah, of course.

CLARA. What color was the canoe?

GUNNER. Blue. Green. Red.

CLARA. It was metallic silver.

GUNNER. *(remembering)* Oh, the Coleman.

CLARA. *(She sighs.)* We were in the Coleman. The sun was goin' down, and the loons were out.

(They all make loon sounds, except GUNNER. KANUTE *mimes like he's going to shoot a loon with a rifle.)*

CLARA. Gunner brought two plastic cups and a bottle of Boone's Farm wine. Strawberry.

BERNICE. Oh, my favorite.

CLARA. He put the ring in the bottom of my cup. It was kinda dark and I almost swallowed it.

BERNICE. So romantic.

GUNNER. Thank you.

CLARA. We held up our cups and Gunner said to me… *(She looks at* GUNNER.*)* You remember what ya said to me?

GUNNER. *(to himself)* Oh, crap. *(to* CLARA*)* Yah, of course I remember.

CLARA. Okay, go ahead.

GUNNER. Okay…I said, Clara…you are the woman who I would really like to be married to, okay, so will you please take my hand in holy matrimony, and stuff.

CLARA. *(astonished)* Oh, my gosh. That's exactly what he said. He remembered.

GUNNER. Really?–

CLARA. Not even close–

GUNNER. Dangit.

KANUTE. Looks like it's up to me. *(Getting on one knee. To* BERNICE*)* Bernice, I will travel to the ends of the earth to earn your love–

BERNICE. *(to* AARVID*)* Yes, I will marry you, Aarvid.

KANUTE. You gotta be kiddin' me! *(Getting up. To* AARVID.*)* Wait, did ya ask her parents first? Do ya have a pre-nup? Is she gonna take your name? All the stuff ya gotta know before ya get married.

BERNICE. We'll figure that stuff out, okay. My parents are fine and I don't need a pre-nup.

KANUTE. Yah, that's cause he's broke. How about religion? What religion are ya?

BERNICE. I'm Lutheran.

AARVID. Me too.

KANUTE. Crap. Ya know, Aarvid, when ya get married, ya can't go out anymore. I mean, what are ya gonna tell all your other women?

BERNICE. What other women?

AARVID. There are no other women.

KANUTE. I know what ya do in Hibbing. I have spies.

BERNICE. What do ya do in Hibbing?

AARVID. Don't listen to him.

KANUTE. C'mon, Bernice. You're the only one that gets me.

BERNICE. I don't get you.

KANUTE. Dangit.

AARVID. That's okay, Kanute. No one gets ya.

KANUTE. Dork.

(The music starts.)

SONG - "The 'Just Got Hosed Over by a Dork' Blues"

(sings)

BERNICE IS GONNA MARRY AN UNEMPLOYED DORK.
HE CAN'T BRING HOME THE BACON, LET ALONE THE PORK.
SOMEHOW HE CONVINCED HER HE WAS BETTER THAN ME.
HE CAN'T EVEN SPEAK

(He cries out in "WOOKIE.")

Aaaaa!
WOOKIE.
WELL, I GOT SIX STORES
AND I HATE TO LOSE.

I GOT THE JUST HOSED OVER BY A DORK, BLUES.

JUST YOU WAIT. AIN'T OVER YET.
BERNICE WILL END UP WITH ME, YOU BET.

*(to **BERNICE**)*

I'M THE ONE WHO'S MEANT FOR YOU.
I OWN A TWO ACRE DEER PETTING ZOO.

AND I OWN SHEEP, THREE DIFFERENT KINDS.
AND I HAVE NO TAN LINES.
That's a bonus.
I'M GONNA TOTALLY MAKE YA CHANGE YOUR MIND.
WHEN I SHOW YA SOME SWEET MOVES THAT I REFINED.
FIRST I'M GONNA GIVE YA ONE OF THESE.

(He makes a goofy dance move.)

THIS ONE WILL BRING YA TO YOUR KNEES.

(He does another goofy dance move.)

THEN I'LL END IT WITH A MOVE I CALL THE GRETZKY.

(He does another goofy dance move.)

HOW CAN ANYONE EVER RESIST ME.

SORRY, AARV, I HATE TO GLOAT.
SHE'S GOIN' FOR THE GUY WITH THE BIGGER BOAT.
SHE'S WITH ME. THE VERDICT'S IN.

(He leans into **BERNICE**.*)*

FOR CHRISTMAS I'LL GIVE YOU A SHEEP SKIN.

ONE MORE THING I'D LIKE TO SAY.
I'M SO HAPPY THAT I CHASED THE
JUST GOT HOSED OVER BY A DORK BLUES
AWAY.

(The song ends.)

So, where do ya wanna go on our honeymoon?

BERNICE. Kanute, listen to me. I want ya to completely clear your mind–

KANUTE. Done.

BERNICE. It's over. I'm sorry. I'm marrying Aarvid.

KANUTE. *(to* **AARVID**) In that case, can I be the best man?

AARVID. Yah, sure, when chickens grow lips.

KANUTE. Well, at least I'm gonna be the Godfather.

CLARA. Undecided.

KANUTE. Dangit.

BERNICE. *(to* **AARVID**) We need to set a date.

AARVID. For what?

BERNICE. For when we're gonna get married. Gah!

AARVID. Oh, yah, I thought we could maybe think about it for awhile, and–

BERNICE. January 5th.

AARVID. That's in three months.

BERNICE. Yah.

AARVID. Well, doesn't it take time to, like, ya know, plan weddings?

BERNICE. Oh, it's already planned. I've been planning it since I was six.

KANUTE. Bernice, why do ya wanna get married so fast all of a sudden?

BERNICE. Cause I want babies. Five of 'em.

AARVID. Five?

BERNICE. Uh huh.

AARVID. Five?

BERNICE. Uh huh.

AARVID. Five?

BERNICE. Uh huh.

> (**AARVID** *holds up his open hand and mouths "five."*
> *She nods.*)

Maybe six.

CLARA. She's got baby fever.

> (*The music starts. She looks at the machine.*)

GUNNER. Let me guess. And you got the cure.

CLARA. Right you are, pork chop. Listen up.

> ***SONG - "Baby Fever"***
>
> (*singing*)
>
> BABIES ON THE FLOOR,
> SHE'LL HAVE SOME BABIES BY THE DOOR.
> SHE'LL HAVE SOME BABIES CRAWLIN' DOWN THE STREET,
> TO PLAY ON THE LAKE SHORE.
>
> SHE'S AN EAGER BEAVER,
> GOT BABY FEVER,
> SHE'LL HAVE FIVE OR SIX OR MORE.

AARVID. Or more?

CLARA.

> BABIES BRING YOU GLEE.
> AS GOOD AS SATELLITE TV.
> AND EVEN THOUGH YOU GET ATROCIOUS GAS
> AND STRETCH MARKS TO YOUR KNEE.
>
> WITH DIAPERS PILED,
> YOU'LL LOVE YOUR CHILD,
> A BRAND NEW MINI-ME.
>
> SO MUCH TO LOOK FOR,
> FEELIN' LIKE YOU'RE LIFTIN' BRICKS,
>
> *(holding her stomach)*
>
> AND THEN YA TOSS ALL YOUR COOKIES,
> BARFIN' WHEN THE BABY KICKS.
>
> SHE'S GOT BABY FEVER,
>
> *(to* **AARVID***)*
>
> YOU WON'T BE GETTIN' ANY
> FOR FIVE YEARS OR SIX.

AARVID. Wait, what?

CLARA.

> BELLY BUTTON'S GONE.
> TOO FAT TO PUT MY RING BACK ON.
> I'M FEELIN' UGLY, UNDESIRABLE.
> I EAT FROM DUSK TILL DAWN.
>
> MY BABY BUMP'S ON STEROIDS,
> GOT RAGING HEMORRHOIDS,
> CAN'T WAIT TIL I SPAWN.
>
> GET READY MOMMA,
> GONNA SET MY BABY FREE.
> CAUSE I AM DONE BEIN' PREGNANT
> GET THIS BABY OUTTA ME.
>
> FEELS LIKE MY BACK WAS TASERED.
> I WEAR DEPENDS CAUSE EVERY TIME I SNEEZE I PEE.
>
> I AM DONE BEIN' PREGNANT,
> WOULD SOMEONE HELP ME GET THIS BABY OUT OF ME.

BERNICE. Wow. That started out bein' kind of a happy song, then it kinda went in a different direction.

CLARA. *(feeling a sharp pain)* Ahh! It's comin'! It's comin'!

GUNNER. *(panicking)* What, the baby?!

CLARA. *(sheepish)* No, it was somethin' else.

(She hurries into the bathroom.)

GUNNER. Not gonna ask.

AARVID. *(to BERNICE)* Ya still wanna have five babies?

BERNICE. Yah, more than ever. And I wanna start right away.

KANUTE. No lesson learned, there.

AARVID. Honey, people don't have five babies anymore. They have two and a half. *(He points to KANUTE.)* Kanute is the half.

KANUTE. Think how great it would be to have five kids. If ya ever need a kidney, it would be like your very own organ farm.

BERNICE. Charming.

KANUTE. Of course *I* would never do that. I mean, if *I* ever needed a kidney, I'd adopt.

(CLARA comes out of the bathroom.)

AARVID. *(changing the subject)* So, Gunner, you must be lookin' forward to havin' a baby, huh?

GUNNER. *(sincere)* Oh, yah. Big time.

BERNICE. I bet ya cry when ya see your baby for the first time.

GUNNER. How much?

CLARA. Gunner doesn't cry.

BERNICE. Really? Never?

CLARA. He was born without tear ducts.

(Laughs then quickly gets sad.)

GUNNER. Funny.

BERNICE. *(to CLARA)* You've never seen Gunner cry?

(CLARA shakes her head, "no.")

That's sad.

CLARA. Gunner doesn't feel sad. He has two emotions, disturbed and indifferent.

GUNNER. That's one of the great things about bein' married. Ya never have to speak for yourself again.

BERNICE. *(looking out the window)* Wow, it's really comin' down out there.

CLARA. *(looking outside, worried)* Where is everyone? They should be here by now.

GUNNER. They'll get here. They're just delayed by the snow.

CLARA. *(concerned)* They're not comin'...All I want is nice things for the baby. Things I never had growin' up. *(she cries)* That's not gonna happen now.

GUNNER. What do ya mean, I made some nice things for the baby.

CLARA. You built an obstacle course.

GUNNER. It's a brutal world out there, okay. He'll need to learn survival skills.

CLARA. Our baby will need love, not survival training.

GUNNER. Are you questioning my parenting decisions?

CLARA. Yah!

KANUTE. Hey, ya still want that gun ya ordered for the baby?

CLARA. You ordered a gun for our baby?

GUNNER. It's just a twenty-two. It's not even a gun.

*(He shoots a look at **KANUTE**.)*

KANUTE. Old Man Hansen brought down a moose with a twenty-two once.

GUNNER. Not helpin'.

CLARA. We are not gettin' our baby a gun!

KANUTE. It's got a little tiny baby grip. He'll be able to shoot it before he can walk.

(He demonstrates, like he's a baby, cocking the gun, firing it, making the sound of a baby gun going off, then the kickback.)

CLARA. *(to* GUNNER*)* I'm goin' for custody.

GUNNER. Oh, come on.

CLARA. *(looking out the window, concerned)* Where is everyone?

GUNNER. They'll be here.

CLARA. My cousin, Lori, is comin' up from the Twin Cities. I haven't seen her in 20 years.

GUNNER. Which cousin is that?

CLARA. Lori Johnson. You haven't met her.

KANUTE. Is she single?

GUNNER. Wait, you have a cousin named Lori Johnson?

CLARA. Yah.

GUNNER. Where'd she grow up?

CLARA. Thunder Bay. Her family moved away when I was a kid. I totally forgot about her.

GUNNER. What are her parents' names?

CLARA. Joe and Shirley. Why?

GUNNER. Cause *I* have a cousin from Thunder Bay named Lori Johnson whose parents are Joe and Shirley.

AARVID. Whoa.

CLARA. Wait, what?

GUNNER. Did Joe run a roofing business?

CLARA. Yah, before they moved away. I don't know what he's doin' now.

GUNNER. And Shirley was a gym teacher?

CLARA. Oh, crap.

KANUTE. Okay, what am I missing?

AARVID. *(To* GUNNER*)* How did that get by ya?

GUNNER. I can't keep track of every Johnson I'm related to.

CLARA. You can't even keep track of your own Johnson.

GUNNER. That's right.

KANUTE. Now, I'm really confused.

BERNICE. Is she a first cousin, or distant?

CLARA. First cousin.

BERNICE. Whoa.

KANUTE. Okay, so Lori Johnson is... *(to* CLARA*) your* cousin and she's also... *(to* GUNNER*) your* cousin?

AARVID. Which means Gunner and Clara are first cousins.

BERNICE. Is that even legal?

> (KANUTE *sings the* Deliverance *banjo song, crossing his eyes.)*

GUNNER. Holy crap. We're gonna have a Kanute baby!

KANUTE. Yes!

AARVID. How could you not know you were related?

CLARA. Well, maybe if Gunner and I talked once in awhile we'd know somethin' about each other.

GUNNER. Nothin' good ever comes out of talkin', okay...It just leads to arguing and then gun play.

AARVID. Okay, so how are you related?

GUNNER. Joe is my dad's brother.

CLARA. And he's my mom's half brother.

BERNICE. So, you two have the same grandfather?

CLARA. Grampa Louie.

GUNNER. I was told he just kinda fell off the map after my grandmother passed away.

CLARA. Yah, well, he remarried, and then he had my mom, and then shortly after that... *(emotional)* He fell into a wood chipper.

> (KANUTE *makes a wood chipper noise, standing behind the table miming that he's putting wood into the wood chipper, pushing the wood down with his leg, his leg gets caught, he gets pulled into the wood chipper, bones grinding, it pulls him down until he disappears behind the table, then he pops his head up, resting it on the table, dead. Everyone just watches him.)*

GUNNER. *(to* KANUTE*)* Ya know, that's surprising even for you.

BERNICE. So, no one figured out you were related at your wedding?

CLARA. We eloped. Cause Gunner is so cheap–

GUNNER. Yah, we already covered that, thank you. So, how did you get in touch with Lori?

CLARA. She called me out of the blue. She heard I was pregnant and she wanted to tell me somethin' so I invited her up to see the baby.

AARVID. That's probly what she wanted to tell ya.

(KANUTE *sings the* Deliverance *banjo song again, crossing his eyes.*)

GUNNER. Would you stop that!

BERNICE. The baby's gonna be fine, okay. If there was a problem the doctor would have seen it on the ultra-sound.

CLARA. Yah, you're probably right.

KANUTE. Hey, look on the bright side, there, Gunner. You're gonna be the proud father of a nephew.

(CLARA *laughs, then she cries.*)

CLARA. (*going to the phone*) I'm gonna call my mom and find out. (*putting the phone to her ear*) No dial tone. That's weird.

KANUTE. I wonder if it's cause of all the snow.

(*He goes downstage to look out the down stage window on the "fourth wall."*)

CLARA. Let's see what's on the radio.

(*She turns the radio on.*)

RADIO (V.O.). We are experiencing a freakishly heavy snow storm here in Bunyan County. All roads are closed. Do not go outside. Stay indoors even if it's an emergency. Like you're outta beer. This is a message from the Bunyan County Broadcast System.

(CLARA *turns it off. She looks frightened.*)

KANUTE. It's the first sign of the apocalypse.

AARVID. (*looking out the downstage window*) It's a snow storm.

KANUTE. That's not a snow storm. That's a tah-snownami! Snowmageddin. A blizzaster. Snowtastrophy. It's the Snowlocaust–

BERNICE. Yah, we get it, Kanute. Lots of snow. Now, knock it off. You're scarin' Clara.

(**CLARA** *is fright-faced.*)

GUNNER. *(looking out the down stage window)* Kanute, where's your car-truck?

KANUTE. *(looking out the window)* It's right out…wait, where is it? Cheese and crackers, my car-truck is gone.

AARVID. It's buried in the snow.

GUNNER. Where's the snowmobile?

AARVID. Buried.

GUNNER. It was right over there. Maybe we can dig it out.

KANUTE. I moved it.

GUNNER. Where?

KANUTE. What am I supposed to have all the answers?

CLARA. I'm gonna have a Kanute baby!

(*She cries.*)

GUNNER. Okay, we can't control that, honey, and right now we have much bigger problems to worry about.

CLARA. Bigger problems?!

BERNICE. *(looking at the book)* The book says any excitement could induce the baby.

GUNNER. Everything's gonna be alright, honey, just…don't have the baby, okay?

CLARA. *(sarcastic)* Oh, yah, no problem, honey, cause I have total control over when the baby arrives.

GUNNER. Ya do?

CLARA. No!

GUNNER. Okay, alright, let's think. We need to relax Clara's…lady place.

(*The music starts.* **CLARA** *sits at the center table.*)

Okay, a song. Good. That'll relax her.

SONG - "Lady Place"

GUNNER.

(sings)

THINK A VERY HAPPY THOUGHT.
KEEPS THE NERVES FROM BEING OVER-WROUGHT.
BEAR IN MIND IT'S NOT A RACE,
KEEP THE BABY IN YOUR LADY PLACE.

KANUTE.

LADY PLACE, LADY PLACE.

GUNNER. (to **CLARA**)

WOULD YOU LIKE AN EASY CHAIR.

(**CLARA** shoots **GUNNER** a look.)

No? Okay.

KANUTE.

LADY PLACE, LADY PLACE.

GUNNER.

LET US KEEP THE BABY THERE.

CLARA. Not helping.

GUNNER.	**KANUTE.**
HOLD THE BABY OFF A DAY.	HOLD, HOLD THE BABY OFF A DAY.
JUST TRY THINKIN' OF A CHEESE SOUFFLE.	JUST THINK OF CHEESE, CHEESE SOUFFLE.
HAPPY THOUGHTS AND COOL FRESH AIR.	HAP HAPPY THOUGHTS AND COOL FRESH AIR
KEEP THE BABY IN YOUR PLACE DOWN THERE.	KEEP IT DOWN THERE.
PLACE DOWN THERE, PLACE DOWN THERE, YOU'RE SO PRETTY I DECLARE.	PLACE DOWN THERE, PLACE DOWN THERE, YOU'RE SO PRETTY I DECLARE.

CLARA. Shut it!

GUNNER.	**KANUTE.**
PLACE DOWN THERE, PLACE DOWN THERE, LET US KEEP THE BABY THERE.	PLACE DOWN THERE, PLACE DOWN THERE, LET US KEEP KEEP IT IN THERE.

GUNNER.	KANUTE.	BERNICE & AARVID.
THINK ABOUT A HAPPY TIME.	THINK THINK ABOUT A HAPPY TIME.	THINK ABOUT HAPPY TIME
CATCHING WALLEYES OR A NURSERY RHYME.	CATCHING WALLEYES NURSERY RHYME.	CATCHING WALLEYES OR NURSERY RHYME.
COUNTING ON YOU IN THE CLUTCH	COUNT COUNTING ON YOU IN THE CLUTCH.	COUNTING ON YOU IN.
KEEP THE BUNNY IN THE RABBIT HUTCH.	KEEP BUNNY IN THE HUTCH.	KEEP BUNNY IN THE HUTCH.
RABBIT HUTCH, RABBIT HUTCH,	RAB RABBIT HUTCH, RAB RABBIT HUTCH.	RAB RABBIT HUTCH. RABBIT HUTCH.
BE THE TORTOISE NOT THE HARE.	BE THE TORTOISE, DON'T BE THE HARE.	TORTOISE. NOT THE HARE.
RABBIT HUTCH, RABBIT HUTCH,	RAB RABBIT HUTCH. RAB RABBIT HUTCH.	RABBIT RABBIT HUTCH.
LET US KEEP THE BUNNY THERE.	LET US KEEP. KEEP IT IN THERE.	LET US KEEP. KEEP IT IN THERE.

(**CLARA** *gets up and goes behind the bar.*)

BERNICE & **KANUTE** & **AARVID** & **GUNNER.**

THINK A VERY HAPPY THOUGHT,
KEEPS THE NERVES FROM BEING OVER-WROUGHT.
BEAR IN MIND IT'S NOT A RACE.
KEEP THE BABY IN YOUR LADY PLACE.

CLARA. *(talking over the music)* My water just broke!

GUNNER. Oh, it's just a false alarm.

CLARA. No, it's for real this time!

KANUTE. *(looking behind the bar)* Clean up on aisle four!

CLARA. I'm goin' into labor!

BERNICE. We won't make it to the hospital!

CLARA. I'm gonna have the baby right here, Gunner, and you're gonna deliver it!

GUNNER. Me?!

CLARA. Yah, you!

KANUTE. He shoulda read the book!

CLARA. Release the Kraken!

> (GUNNER *faints. Everyone looks at him.*)

> *(blackout)*

END OF ACT I

ACT II

(**GUNNER** *is sitting on the left side of the stage center table.* **CLARA** *is sitting at the same table on the right side.* **BERNICE, AARVID** *and* **KANUTE** *are standing around them.*)

(**GUNNER** *looks like he's seen a ghost. He rocks back and forth in his chair mumbling something to himself.*)

(*Lights up. The music starts.* **BERNICE, KANUTE** *and* **AARVID** *do a country line dance to the song.*)

SONG - "Knee Deep"

BERNICE. *(sings)*

CLARA IS HAVIN' HER A BABY SUPERSTAR.
SHE'S GONNA HAVE IT.

KANUTE & AARVID.

HAVE IT.

BERNICE.

RIGHT HERE IN THIS BAR.
GUNNER IS NERVOUS, SITTIN' ROCKIN' AS HE CHANTS.

WILL HE COME THRU?

KANUTE & AARVID.

COME THRU.

BERNICE.

OR WILL HE CRAP HIS PANTS.
WILL HE COME THRU,

(to **CLARA***)*

FOR BABY AND YOU,
OR WILL HE TAKE OFF ON HIS OLD SKIDOO?

GUNNER DON'T QUIT, YOU'RE SCARED LET'S ADMIT.
AND NOW YOU ARE KNEE DEEP IN–

KANUTE & AARVID. *(spoken)* WHOA!

BERNICE. Sorry.

> WILL GUNNER FIND THE DOOR
> OR WILL HE COME ABOUT.
> WILL HE COME THRU

KANUTE & AARVID.

> OR FAINT

BERNICE.

> LIKE A GIRLY SCOUT.

> *(**GUNNER** takes lipstick out of **CLARA**'s purse, and gets ready to apply it on his lips.)*

> CLARA SHE NEEDS HER MAN
> THERE'S NO MORE FOOLIN' ROUND, SO,

> *(to **GUNNER**, taking away the purse and lipstick)*

> GIVE ME YOUR PURSE AND PUT YOUR LIPSTICK DOWN.
> WILL HE NOT CARE,
> TAKE OFF IN THIN AIR,
> OR WILL GUNNER FINALLY GROW A PAIR.

> *(**KANUTE** goes behind the bar and drops down out of sight.)*

> GUNNER DON'T QUIT,

> *(**CLARA** gets up.)*

CLARA. It's comin'.

BERNICE.

> YOU'RE SCARED LET'S ADMIT.

> *(**CLARA** goes behind the bar.)*

CLARA. Gunner, I need ya.

BERNICE.

> AND NOW YOU ARE KNEE DEEP,

> *(**CLARA** groans.)*

> AND NOW YOU ARE KNEE DEEP,

> *(**CLARA** groans.)*

> AND NOW YOU ARE KNEE DEEP IN…

(*CLARA groans one last time,* KANUTE *pops his head above the bar. He's wearing a baby costume with bonnet, rattle and bottle.*)

KANUTE. Daddy!

GUNNER. Nooooooo!

(*blackout*)

(GUNNER *is lying on the floor in the same place he was at the end of the first act when he fainted.* CLARA *is sitting in a chair, leaning back, trying to keep it together.* BERNICE, KANUTE *and* AARVID *are kneeling around* GUNNER, *fanning him.*)

(*Lights up.*)

GUNNER. (*cont.*) Noooooooo!

BERNICE. Gunner, wake up…Come on, Gunner, wake up.

GUNNER. (*waking up*) What happened?

BERNICE. Ya fainted.

GUNNER. I had the weirdest dream.

(*pointing to* BERNICE, *channeling Dorothy in* The Wizard of Oz)

You were there,

(*pointing to* AARVID)

and you were there,

(*pointing to* KANUTE)

and you're an idiot.

KANUTE. What was the dream about?

GUNNER. Well, Clara's water broke and she was gonna have the baby in the bar and I was gonna have to deliver it.

CLARA. It wasn't a dream, Gunner. I'm in labor, the baby's comin', and you're gonna deliver it. (*She feels a twinge of pain.*) Ah!

GUNNER. Okay. Alrighty, then.

(GUNNER *starts to faint again.*)

CLARA. Don't let him faint. Keep him awake.

GUNNER. I'm not fainting, I just need a Kit Kat Bar. Maybe a hamburger. And a shot of tequila.

(KANUTE *goes behind the bar.*)

CLARA. No tequila. I need you alert for this.

GUNNER. Ya know, I think you're gonna be just fine on your own, there, honey. I'm gonna just take a little nap, here. Why don't ya go ahead and wake me when I'm a daddy.

CLARA. Gunner, don't you dare fall asleep!

KANUTE. I can help deliver it.

(*He comes out from behind the bar wearing yellow rubber kitchen gloves, holding a measuring tape.*)

CLARA. No, thanks.

KANUTE. C'mon, it's not my first trip to the rodeo. My cat had babies. A whole mess of 'em.

BERNICE. Ya mean "litter."

KANUTE. Oh, no, it was a mess…Do not use salad tongs.

BERNICE. (*gross*) Ohh.

(KANUTE *approaches* CLARA *with the measuring tape. He opens it about three feet and holds it up to* CLARA*'s pelvis.*)

CLARA. What are ya doin'?

KANUTE. We gotta see how dilated you are.

CLARA. Get that away from me. (*feeling a sharp pain*) Ahh!

GUNNER. What was that?

CLARA. (*in pain*) A contraction.

GUNNER. Is that bad?

CLARA. (*Still in pain, she looks at her watch.*) I'm in labor, and if you went to Lamaze class, you'd know.

KANUTE. (*holding the book* Pregnancy for Dummies) It says in the book here, it could be false labor.

CLARA. (*in pain*) Do I look like I'm fakin' it?!–

GUNNER. Okay, okay, we're all under a lot of stress, here.

BERNICE. Clara, you are a woman warrior. I wanna be just like you when I get old. *(realizing her mistake)* Older. Slightly. Not even. More mature. Yah, more mature, that's it.

AARVID. Hey, let's see if there's any news.

(He points to the radio. CLARA turns it on. KANUTE goes to the down stage window and looks out.)

RADIO. *(V.O.)* I repeat, all roads are closed. With up to four feet of snow in some areas, this is the worst snow disaster in the history of Bunyan County. And that's really sayin' somethin' cause it snows a lot here. Again, do not go outside.

(CLARA turns it off.)

KANUTE. I can't breathe. All that snow. Everything's closing in on me. I can't take it much longer.

BERNICE. He's gettin' cabin fever.

CLARA. He's only been here an hour. He's here, like, five hours a day and *now* he gets cabin fever?

KANUTE. I've never been to the Grand Casino in Hinckley.

CLARA. *(looking up)* Please don't let it be a Kanute baby. *(to GUNNER)* Do ya think we're related?

GUNNER. We can't worry about that now, honey.

KANUTE. I gotta bad feelin' about this. A real bad feelin'. *(He whispers.)* We're stuck.

(The music starts.)

CLARA. *(re: the music)* Oh, for the love of corn muffins, he's gonna sing again.

SONG - "Stuck in a Snow Storm"

KANUTE. *(sings)*
STUCK IN A SNOW STORM.
A GIANT SNOW STORM.
THE WORLD IS OUTTA TILT
AND ONE OF US WILL DIE.

KANUTE.

>WHICH ONE WILL BE THE WEAKEST
>HELPLESS ONE AMONG US.
>IT WON'T BE ME
>I'M WAY TOO YOUNG TO SAY GOODBYE.

AARVID. No, you're not.

KANUTE.

>IT'S LIKE THE AIRPLANE
>CRASH IN THE ANDES.
>THE SOCCER TEAM WAS LOST
>IN MOUNTAINOUS FRONTIER.

>THEY HAD TO EAT EACH OTHER
>SO THEY COULD SURVIVE IT.
>I THINK WE ALL COULD LIVE
>ON GUNNER FOR A YEAR.

>I HEAR HE TASTES LIKE SQUID.
>AND PARTLY CHICKEN.
>A HINT OF CHICKEN.

>I WOULD NOT EAT AARVID.
>CAUSE HE WOULD TASTE JUST LIKE
>RESENTMENT AND FAILURE.

>WE'LL NEED A LEADER.
>TO KEEP THE ORDER.
>I KNOW THE PERSON, CLARA,
>WE CAN ALL AGREE.

>OH, WAIT, WE CAN'T ELECT HER
>SHE MIGHT DIE IN CHILD BIRTH.

CLARA. Dork.

KANUTE.

>I KNOW THE PERFECT PERSON
>HUMBLE SERVANT ME.

>I'LL NEED TO FIND A MATE.
>SOMEONE WHO FISHES.
>AND WASHES DISHES.
>SOMEONE TO PROCREATE.
>I CHOOSE BERNICE TO MAKE
>A NEW WORLD OF KANUTES.

BERNICE. No, thanks.

KANUTE.

NOT YOUR DECISION.

BERNICE. Why?

KANUTE.

THERE'S A REVISION.

BERNICE. What?

KANUTE.

I CHANGED THE CONSTITUTION
SO YOU'D BE MY WIFE.

BERNICE. Not.

KANUTE.

WE'LL BE THE KING AND QUEEN,
THE RULERS OF KANUTEVILLE.
TOGETHER WE WILL START A NEW,
TOGETHER WE WILL START A NEW,

(*He looks at the machine, it's skipping.*)

TOGETHER WE WILL START A NEW

(**AARVID** *hits the machine. It stops skipping.*)

KANUTEVILLE LIFE.

AARVID. He's goin' *Lord of the Flies* on us.

KANUTE. (*to the others*) We need to make a decision on Gunner. C'mon, who's with me? No one has to find out. We just hit him over the head with a shovel–

GUNNER. You're not gonna hit me with a shovel, okay. No one wants that, do they, Clara.

(**CLARA** *thinks a little too long.*)

Clara?

CLARA. I'm thinkin'.

AARVID. (*changing the subject*) You ready to deliver a baby, big guy?

GUNNER. We need a doctor. (*lifting up the phone*) Dangit, the phone is still out.

BERNICE. Anyone have a cell phone?

AARVID. *(looking at his cell phone)* No signal.

KANUTE. We're cut off. It's the end of the world.

GUNNER. I got snow shoes. I'll hike out, get a doctor, and bring him back.

KANUTE. How do ya know everyone's not dead?

AARVID. He's goin' to the dark side.

> *(KANUTE starts to do gentle karate chops on GUNNER's shoulders.)*

GUNNER. What are ya doin'?

KANUTE. Tenderizing.

GUNNER. Knock it off!

KANUTE. In case we have to kill one of us, I have a gun.

CLARA. On you?

KANUTE. No, I keep it behind the toilet tank in the bathroom.

> *(He hums a few bars from the theme to* The Godfather.*)*

BERNICE. *(taking that in)* We gotta go for help.

KANUTE. You heard him. No one go outside. There might be a snowvalanche.

AARVID. A "snowvalanche?"

KANUTE. Yah, it's like an avalanche, only with snow.

AARVID. An avalanche already has snow.

KANUTE. *(thinks)* I'm gonna look that up.

> *(We hear a loud creaking sound. Everyone looks up to the roof.)*

CLARA. What was that?

GUNNER. Sounded like the roof.

AARVID. The snow is puttin' weight on it.

CLARA. We should be okay. We got a four foot test roof.

BERNICE. What's that?

CLARA. The roof will hold up to four feet of snow before cavin' in.

GUNNER. Yah, about that, honey, umm…I went with the two foot test roof.

CLARA. You what?

GUNNER. Do you know how expensive a four foot test roof is?!

BERNICE. Didn't it say we were gettin' four feet of snow?

GUNNER. Only in some areas.

(The roof creaks again. Everyone reacts.)

CLARA. Okay, let me understand this. We're all gonna die cause you went cheap on the roof?

GUNNER. I got a roof rake, okay. I'll just go outside and rake the snow off the roof. Problem solved.

CLARA. Could anything else go wrong?

GUNNER. No. Nothin'. I'll just go outside and– *(looking out the down stage window)* are those wolves?

(We hear a wolf howl.)

CLARA. Are you kiddin' me?

(Everyone looks out the down stage window.)

BERNICE. Oh, my gosh.

AARVID. Holy shizzle.

KANUTE. Must be the wolf scent.

GUNNER. The what?

KANUTE. A case of wolf scent broke in the back of my car-truck.

GUNNER. Why do you have wolf scent?!

KANUTE. To attract wolves. Duh!

(We hear a wolf howl.)

CLARA. My life is flashin' before my eyes. *(She feels a sharp pain.)* Ahh! *(She looks at her watch.)*

BERNICE. *(holding the book)* It says in the book that stress is bad for her, Gunner. You need to say somethin' to calm her. Somethin' *loving*.

GUNNER. Yah, sure, okay, umm... *(to* **CLARA***)* Ya need anything?

CLARA. *(rolling her eyes)* We need clean towels and boiling water.

GUNNER. What are we gonna do? Boil the baby?!

CLARA. Oh, for rice cakes.

BERNICE. I'll do it.

(BERNICE goes into the kitchen.)

CLARA. And we'll need a scissors. Someone has to cut the umbilical cord.

KANUTE. *(to GUNNER)* Flip ya for it.

CLARA. And I'll need some ice chips.

GUNNER. Good idea. I'll make ya a Margarita.

CLARA. Boy, it's a good thing men don't have babies.

(The music starts. BERNICE comes out of the kitchen.)

GUNNER. That's it, sing. Yah. It'll take your mind off it.

SONG - "If Men Had Babies, We'd All Be Extinct"

CLARA. *(sings)*

> GOIN' INTO LABOR,
> THINK I NEED A SHRINK,
> HUSBAND WANTS TO BOIL THE BABY
> THEN MAKE ME A DRINK.
>
> DOESN'T GIVE ME CONFIDENCE,
> LET ME BE SUCCINCT.
> IF MEN HAD BABIES,
> WE'D ALL BE EXTINCT.

BERNICE. Amen!

GUNNER.

> WOMEN ARE UNGRATEFUL,
> MEN DO LOTS OF THINGS.

KANUTE. Mmm Hmm.

GUNNER.

> JUST THE OTHER DAY
> I TIED YOUR TIMBERLAND BOOT STRINGS.

AARVID. Sing it, brother!

GUNNER.

> INSTEAD OF BEIN' GRATEFUL,
> SHE TURNS TO ME AND SINGS,

CLARA.

YOU ARE THE ASS BENEATH MY WINGS.

AARVID. Really?

GUNNER. Yah!

GUNNER & AARVID & KANUTE.

UNGRATEFUL.

CLARA & BERNICE.

EXTINCT.

GUNNER & AARVID & KANUTE.

UNGRATEFUL.

CLARA & BERNICE.

EXTINCT.

GUNNER & AARVID & KANUTE.

UNGRATEFUL.

GUNNER.

YOU KNOW, MEN HAVE FEELINGS, TOO.

AARVID. Preach!

CLARA.

SO DO WOLVES,

LIKE THOSE OUTSIDE PACING AROUND.

WAITING FOR OUR ROOF TO COME DOWN.

(**CLARA** *looks very stressed.*)

BERNICE & AARVID & KANUTE.

CLARA IS

A LITTLE STRESSED.

SHE JUST NEEDS,

SOME TENDERNESS.

GUNNER.

I WILL SHOW YOU I CAN BE OF WORTH.

I WILL COME THRU FOR THE BIRTH.

CLARA. Seriously?

GUNNER. Yah.

CLARA & BERNICE.

HALLELU!

GUNNER & AARVID & KANUTE.

AMEN.

CLARA & BERNICE.
> HALLELU!

GUNNER & AARVID & KANUTE.
> AMEN.

CLARA & BERNICE.
> HALLELU!

CLARA & BERNICE & AARVID & KANUTE.
> GUNNER'S FINALLY COMIN' THRU!

BERNICE & AARVID & KANUTE.
> GOOD NEWS IS
> THERE'S JUST ONE MORE THING TO DO.
> TURN TO CLARA AND SAY "I LOVE YOU."

GUNNER. Say what?

BERNICE & AARVID & KANUTE.
> I LOVE YOU.

GUNNER. Again?

BERNICE & AARVID & KANUTE.
> I LOVE YOU.

GUNNER. Oh, crap.

BERNICE & AARVID & KANUTE.
> I LOVE YOU.
> GUNNER'S FINALLY COMIN' THRU.
> THREE SIMPLE WORDS WILL TURN EVERYTHING AROUND.
> SAY THEM, IT'S SUCH A LOVELY SOUND.
> GUNNER, LET US BE SUCCINCT.
> SAY THEM OR YOU'LL BE EXTINCT.

> *(**BERNICE** goes into the kitchen.)*

CLARA. Well?

GUNNER. Okay, first of all, sayin' that stuff is private, okay, and second of all, men provide lots of value, alright.

CLARA. I'm not sayin' women are more valuable than men, even though mankind would cease to exist without women.

GUNNER. Well, who would fight the wars? Huh?

CLARA. There wouldn't be wars if it was just women.

KANUTE. Instead they would have pillow fights in their panties and bras.

(KANUTE, GUNNER and AARVID stare out, visualizing the pillow fight.)

CLARA. Hellooo!

(GUNNER gives CLARA a, "What did I do?" look. We hear a wolf howl.)

GUNNER. They can't get in, okay. This place is real sturdy.

(The roof creaks and the lights flicker, then stay on.)

CLARA. *(shoots a look at GUNNER)* I'm gonna turn the heat up. Maybe it'll melt the snow off the roof.

(She goes into the kitchen.)

KANUTE. *(staring straight ahead, in a trance)* When I was in the Nam, I survived on rats.

GUNNER. You were never in the Nam.

KANUTE. I visualized it.

AARVID. *(ignoring KANUTE)* Ya know, it's impressive that you and Clara have been together so long. How do ya do it?

GUNNER. *(looking out the down stage window, concerned)* Oh, I just remind myself that marriage isn't a sprint. It's a marathon.

AARVID. I ran a marathon once. I was only happy when it was over.

KANUTE. *(standing right next to GUNNER)* I'm as hungry as a wood tick.

(He does a Hannibal Lector, liver and fava beans, slurp.)

GUNNER. *(Ignoring KANUTE. To AARVID.)* So, are ya havin' second thoughts?

(KANUTE stares at GUNNER.)

AARVID. No, it's just that…Okay, how do ya know when you're ready to get married?

GUNNER. Simple. When you can no longer dress yourself or speak on your own behalf.

AARVID. Great.

GUNNER. Do ya have a favorite color?

AARVID. Yah.

GUNNER. You won't.

AARVID. I think I'm gonna be sick.

(*He heads toward the bathroom.*)

GUNNER. I'll hold your hair.

(**AARVID** *stops and looks back at* **GUNNER.** **GUNNER** *stops.*)

Yah, I don't know where that came from.

KANUTE. It came from my next meal. Gobble, gobble, gobble.

(*Ignoring* **KANUTE,** **AARVID** *and* **GUNNER** *go into the bathroom as* **CLARA** *and* **BERNICE** *come out of the kitchen.* **KANUTE** *stands outside the bathroom, looking in.*)

BERNICE. So, Clara, what do you think the secret is to marriage?

CLARA. Never give up. Yah. It's the anticipation that some day he might do somethin' right that keeps the relationship alive. I mean, even a blind squirrel can find an acorn once in awhile.

KANUTE. (*to* **CLARA**) You have any ketchup?

CLARA. Yah, in the fridge, why?

KANUTE. It's for Gunner. He'll taste better.

(*He goes into the kitchen making a Hannibal Lector slurping sound.*)

BERNICE. Ya ever do anything to spice up the relationship, ya know, like fantasies or role playing?

CLARA. I often pretend that Gunner is someone else.

BERNICE. Ever think about gettin' a divorce?

CLARA. Oh, yah, lots of times. Ya know, when I said, "Till death do us part," I didn't realize I was settin' a goal.

BERNICE. (*sarcastic*) Ya ever think about motivational speaking?

CLARA. *(feels a sharp pain)* Aaah! *(She looks at her watch; in pain.)* Contractions are eight minutes apart. We better get ready. *(groans)* Aah!

(KANUTE comes out of the kitchen with a bottle of ketchup. We hear the roof creak. Looking up, CLARA and BERNICE go into the kitchen as GUNNER and AARVID come back in from the bathroom.)

KANUTE. *(looking at GUNNER)* Gunner...The other white meat.

AARVID. *(Ignoring KANUTE. To GUNNER.)* So, do ya love Clara?

(KANUTE stares at GUNNER)

GUNNER. Ya know, true love is really just a fantasy, okay. I mean, ya find someone ya love, ya marry 'em, ya live with 'em your entire life, then ya watch 'em die. And the winner gets a check from State Farm...That's the best case scenario.

(KANUTE suddenly hurries into the bathroom while looking at GUNNER)

KANUTE. *(while crossing to the bathroom:)* I'm not here, I'm not here, I'm not here.

(He disappears into the bathroom.)

AARVID. *(ignoring KANUTE).* Isn't havin' a baby supposed to help the relationship?

GUNNER. You're askin' me?

AARVID. *(grabbing the book)* Let's see what the book says, here. *(He leafs through it.)* Alright, let's see here...havin' babies...

(The music starts.)

Okay, here.

(Reading from the book. He sings.)

SONG - "When You Have Babies"

AARVID.

> WHEN YOU HAVE BABIES YOUR LIFE WILL FOREVER
>   CHANGE,
> NOTHING WILL BE THE SAME.

GUNNER. I know.

AARVID.

> GETTING NO SLEEP AT NIGHT, BURPING THE BABY RIGHT,
> AND NO TIME TO WATCH THE GAME.

GUNNER. That's in there?

AARVID.

> CRYING, THERE'S CRYING, THEN THERE'S MORE CRYING,
> THE BABY CRIES ALL THE TIME.

GUNNER. You're kiddin', right?

AARVID.

> WHEN IT'S NOT CRYING, IT'S EATING OR POOPING,
> THEN CRYING THE REST OF THE TIME.

GUNNER. It doesn't say that.

AARVID.

> WILL HE BE FROLICKY, WILL HE BE COLLICKY,
> WILL HE WEAR FAKE OR FUR.

GUNNER. Wait, what?

AARVID.

> WILL HE GET CHICKEN POX, WILL HE BE DUMB AS ROCKS,
> OR WILL HE BE A CROSS DRESSER.

GUNNER. Oh, for crap sake.

AARVID.

> SPEND ALL YOUR MONEY ON BABY TWADDLE,
> YOU'LL NEED A SECOND JOB.

GUNNER. What?

AARVID.

> NO HUNTING TRIPS, NO TIME FOR YOUR CARD GAME,
> YOUR LIFE WILL BE ALL SPONGEBOB.

GUNNER. Sponge who?

AARVID.

> GET USED TO PAMPERING CLARA ALL NIGHT AND DAY,
> UNTIL AT LEAST JULY.

GUNNER. That's nine more months.

AARVID.

SHE'LL HAVE ANXIETY, YOU'LL NEED SOBRIETY,
SO KISS YOUR MAN CAVE GOOD BYE.

GUNNER. Not my man cave.

AARVID.

ALL THINGS TO HER WILL BE IRRITATIONS,
DISCOMFORT YOU CAN'T IGNORE.
SWEATING AT NIGHT, HAIR LOSS AND DEPRESSION,
TEETHING MAKES THE NIPPLES SORE.

KANUTE. *(popping his head out of the bathroom)* Did he–

GUNNER. "Snapple." He said "Snapple."

AARVID.

EVERYTHING STOPS WHEN YOU HAVE A BABY.
IT LOOKS LIKE YOUR LIFE IS DONE.

GUNNER. Great.

AARVID.

SO MANY GOOD THINGS ONCE IT'S DELIVERED.
IF ONLY I COULD FIND JUST ONE.
I CAN NOT EVEN FIND JUST ONE.

(The song ends. **GUNNER** *and* **AARVID** *stare straight ahead, despondent.)*

GUNNER. That book sucks.

AARVID. Big time.

(A wolf howls.)

*(***CLARA*** *comes out of the kitchen in pain.)*

CLARA. What's goin' on out here?

GUNNER. Aarvid is havin' second thoughts.

AARVID. I'm just a little confused, that's all.

*(***KANUTE*** *comes out of the bathroom wearing a chef hat and a bib tied around his neck, holding two carving knives, sharpening them.)*

KANUTE. *(imitating Julia Child)* Guess who's comin' to dinner!

CLARA. Kanute! Out!

KANUTE. *(as he goes back into the bathroom:)* Save the giblets.

CLARA. *(to* **AARVID***)* You're confused?

AARVID. I mean, I just lost my job, alright. I'm gonna get another one, okay, a really good one, but right now money is, ya know, kind of an issue.

CLARA. You don't need money as long as you have love. *(She can't keep a straight face, and starts laughing.)* I couldn't land it.

AARVID. *(to* **GUNNER***)* Would you take a bullet for Clara?

GUNNER. Oooh.

CLARA. Oh, this should be good.

GUNNER. What kinda gun, like a B-B gun?

AARVID. No.

GUNNER. A pellet gun?

AARVID. No, a real gun. With a real bullet.

GUNNER. Ya mean, like it grazes me?

AARVID. No.

GUNNER. Maybe hits me in the butt?

AARVID. Would you die for Clara?

GUNNER. Would the death be permanent?

CLARA. Oh, just forget it. *(She feels a twinge of pain.)* Look, when two people are in love like when Gunner and I used to be, it's really great. You'll have a few good years… *(She can't come up with anything else that's good.)* Yah, that's all I got.

AARVID. I don't know, it's all comin' at me so fast. I mean, Bernice has been plannin' this wedding since she was, like, ya know, Little Miss Muffet,

(The music starts.)

…and she wants five babies right now, and…Ya know, maybe I should go have a talk with Bernice.

(He stands up.)

*(***BERNICE** *comes out of the kitchen wearing a very sexy dress.)*

BERNICE, *(in her sexiest voice)* Did someone call me?

AARVID. *(Re:* **BERNICE***'s sexy dress.)* Holy hotdish.

GUNNER. That's for sure.

*(***AARVID*** sits back down.)*

SONG - "Little Miss Muffet"

BERNICE. *(doing a seductive dance, singing)*
JACK, HE WAS NIMBLE, JACK WAS QUICK.
JACK HE JUMPED OVER THE CANDLESTICK.
IF JACK HAD SOME SECOND THOUGHTS HE LEARNED.
HESITATE AND YOUR BUTT IS BURNED.

THEY SAY PETER PETER PUMPKIN EATER
HE HAD HIMSELF A WIFE AND COULDN'T KEEP HER.
IF YA TRY TO PUT ME IN A PUMPKIN SHELL,
I'LL LEAVE YOU FOR THE FARMER IN THE DELL.
IF YOU'RE BAD DON'T BE VERY.
AND IF YOU'RE VERY GOOD YOU WILL FIND
THIS MARY MARY WILL NEVER BE CONTRARY.

*(***BERNICE*** dances.* **KANUTE** *comes out of the bathroom with a dollar bill in his mouth, and one in each hand, walking toward* **BERNICE***.)*

CLARA. Kanute!

*(***KANUTE*** turns and goes back into the bathroom.)*

BERNICE.
JACK AND JILL WENT UP A SCARY HILL.
HUMPTY DUMPTY TOOK A WICKED SPILL.
WHILE ALL THE KINGS HORSES TRIED TO PUT HIM BACK
I WAS FALLIN' FOR YOU LIKE BO PEEP ON CRACK.

LITTLE MISS MUFFET GOT SCARED AWAY.
WHILE SITTIN' ON HER TUFFET EATIN' CURDS AND WHEY.
WELL, POP GOES THE WEASEL WITH MY FIANCE
WHEN I GIVE YOU SOME TUFFET ON OUR WEDDING DAY.

(She sits on **AARVID***'s lap.* **KANUTE** *steps out of the bathroom to watch.)*

BERNICE.

> THIS LITTLE PIGGY ON OUR WEDDING DAY.
> GOOSEY GOOSEY GANDER ON OUR WEDDING DAY.
> HEY DIDDLE DIDDLE ON OUR WEDDING DAY.
> RUB A DUB DUB ON OUR WEDDING DAY.
> WEE WILLIE WINKIE–

GUNNER. Okay, we get it!

BERNICE.

> ON OUR WEDDING DAY.
>
> *(The song ends. To* **AARVID.***)* What did ya wanna talk to me about?

AARVID. Nothin'.

KANUTE. She makes my naughty parts tingle.

CLARA. Kanute!

> *(She points to the bathroom.* **KANUTE** *slinks back into the bathroom.)*

BERNICE. *(She gets up, off his lap.)* Aarvid, will you help me with somethin' in the kitchen?

AARVID. Ya know, I think I'm gonna just sit here for awhile.

BERNICE. I love you.

AARVID. I love you, too.

BERNICE. I love you more than fried cheese curds.

GUNNER. Oh, for crackin' the walnuts!

> *(***KANUTE** *steps out of the bathroom with a brown paper bag over his head with two holes cut out for eye holes and a third mouth hole. He's holding a plunger on his shoulder like he's marching with a rifle.)*

KANUTE. *(chanting like the Witch's guards in* The Wizard of Oz*)* Oh-wee-oh, Guh-nner. Oh-wee-oh, Guh-nner.

CLARA. I will put you outside!

KANUTE. *(channeling the Elephant Man)* I am not an animal!

CLARA. Go!

> *(***KANUTE** *turns and goes back into the bathroom.)*

(We hear a wolf howl.)

GUNNER. *(re: the wolves)* Maybe I should go scare 'em away. Kanute has a gun, right?

BERNICE. *(looking out the upstage window)* There's a wolf right outside the door.

CLARA. No, don't go out there. We're fine as long as the roof holds up. *(The roof creaks. Hopeful.)* The heat will melt the snow, right? *(anxious)* Right? *(She feels a sharp pain.)* Ahh!

BERNICE. Clara's gettin' anxious. Say somethin' to her, Gunner.

AARVID. Three simple words, Gunner. "I," then the "L" word, "you."

GUNNER. I told ya it's a private thing, okay. Ya say stuff like that in public, it just leads to holding hands.

AARVID. I think we need an intervention.

GUNNER. A what?

AARVID. We need to form a love circle around Gunner and let him know he's in a safe zone. C'mon, everyone, group hug.

GUNNER. There will be no hugging!

AARVID. There's a reason you have a hard time expressin' your feelin's Gunner, and we're gonna find out what it is and help ya express 'em.

CLARA. Good luck.

AARVID. You can say it, Gunner. C'mon, I'll show ya how. Gunner, I love you.

GUNNER. Stop it!

AARVID. I love you Gunner. I really love you.

GUNNER. *(plugging his ears, trying to maintain manliness)* Vikings, Vikings, Vikings.

KANUTE. *(Coming out of the bathroom, holding a bottle of Chianti and a bag of fava beans. Like a zombie:)* We found Gunner's kryptonite. The word "love." It'll make him weak. Then we can overpower him, and eat him. *(He walks toward **GUNNER** like a zombie.)* Love, love, love–

BERNICE. *(grabbing* **KANUTE** *by the shirt)* Kanute, snap out of it!

KANUTE. *(He doesn't snap out of it.)* Love, love–

BERNICE. I love you!

KANUTE. *(quickly snapping out of it)* Ya do?

BERNICE. No.

KANUTE. Crap. *(He looks at the Chianti and fava beans.)* What am I doin' with Chianti and fava beans?

AARVID. *(to* **GUNNER***)* You're gonna tell your child ya love him, right?

GUNNER. My parents never told me, and *I* turned out okay.

CLARA. Wow!

GUNNER. Honey, you know how I feel about ya, okay.

CLARA. No, I don't. How do ya feel about me?

GUNNER. *(thinks)* Strongly.

CLARA. I love you, Gunner. You got 5 seconds to respond…4, 3, 2–

GUNNER. I love you. There, I said it.

CLARA. I don't believe you.

GUNNER. Oh, for, pokin' the bear.

CLARA. You just said it to get it over with. It wasn't with meaning.

GUNNER. Look, this is how I am, okay. It's how I grew up. My dad was like that and my parents have been married forever. I don't see what the big deal is.

AARVID. Hmmm. Ya know, I think we need to take baby steps, here, Gunner. I think you need to start with askin' Clara out on a date, ya know, like when ya first met her.

KANUTE. Ya need a good opening line, there, Gunner. Somethin' to get Clara's interest. Here. *(to* **GUNNER***)* Are you an angel? Cause it sure smells like somebody died–

GUNNER. Okay.

CLARA. *(feeling a sharp pain)* Ahhh! *(She looks at her watch. In pain.)* Seven minutes. Keep talkin'. It'll take my mind off it.

(The roof creaks and the lights flicker, then go out, except for a few emergency lights.)

GUNNER. Oh, crap.

CLARA. The heat over-loaded the system.

BERNICE. I'll turn the heat off and flip the circuit breaker.

(She goes into the kitchen. To **GUNNER.***)*

Think of something.

GUNNER. I'm thinkin'.

AARVID. *(changing the subject)* So, Gunner, did you, ahh, have a happy childhood?

GUNNER. *(looking out the window)* Yah, it was fine. Strict, but whatever. It was good.

AARVID. Do you believe in spankin' your child?

GUNNER. Sure, why not?

(The lights go back on. Everyone notices. **BERNICE** *comes out of the kitchen.)*

CLARA. We're not spankin' our baby.

GUNNER. Well, then how do we discipline it?

CLARA. We'll give it a time out.

GUNNER. Oh, for drivin' Miss Daisy. Spanking is fine, okay. It builds character. My dad spanked me so hard with a yard stick I can measure stuff with my butt.

BERNICE. I heard that spankin' might close the child off emotionally.

GUNNER. Well, it didn't do that to me.

CLARA. Oh, my gosh!

AARVID. Gunner, I'm pretty sure you're a good hearted guy, but times are changin'. You're gonna have a baby and it'll need love and affection. It's time to change the cycle, there, buddy, and I know how you can start. Renew your wedding vows with Clara.

GUNNER. Oh, for cryin' in the beer nuts.

CLARA. You're wastin' your time, Aarvid.

KANUTE. *(looking at the book)* I think we need an empathy belly for Gunner.

GUNNER. What's that?

KANUTE. *(He grabs a balloon from the wall.)* Somethin' to feel what it's like to be pregnant. So you can see what Clara is goin' thru and appreciate her for bein' the smokin' hot pregnant baby mamma that she is. Yowza!

(He hands the balloon to **GUNNER.***)*

Here, put it under your shirt.

(We hear a wolf howl.)

GUNNER. Ya know, I think we got bigger issues to deal with right now.

KANUTE. Oh, come on, do it for your wife.

CLARA. He won't do it.

GUNNER. Alright, fine. *(**GUNNER** reluctantly puts it under his shirt.)* Are ya happy?

(He goes behind the bar.)

CLARA. *(She groans from a twinge of pain.)* Now all he has to do is add 30 pounds to it, wear it for three more months, and then pass a kidney stone.

GUNNER. Okay, I get it. Bein' pregnant is difficult. It's just that–

(Suddenly, the balloon pops.)

KANUTE. You killed it!

GUNNER. *(to **CLARA**)* Okay, fine. You win. You're a better parent than me. Just one more thing that Clara can do better.

BERNICE. Oh, she can't write her name in the snow.

*(She looks at **CLARA** who nods, "yes.")*

Okay, never mind.

AARVID. Gunner, it's not a competition, okay. Clara has a bun in the oven and she needs your support right now, alright. She needs all of our support.

(*AARVID hands* **GUNNER** *another balloon. The music starts. Off the music cue,* **AARVID**, **BERNICE** *and* **KANUTE** *enthusiastically put balloons under their shirts.* **GUNNER** *reluctantly puts it under his shirt.* **GUNNER** *doesn't join in at first.*)

SONG - "Bun In The Oven"

BERNICE & KANUTE & AARVID.

SHE GOT A BUN IN THE OVEN.
SHE GOT A BUN IN THE OVEN.

CLARA.

I'M MAKIN' BREAD IN MY BELLY,
HOLD THE LUNCHEON MEAT.
I GOTTA BUN IN THE OVEN AND IT
AIN'T WHOLE WHEAT.

(*They all do the pregnant lady rap dance.* **AARVID** *encourages* **GUNNER** *to join in. He reluctantly does. During the song* **GUNNER** *gets more and more into it.*)

KANUTE & AARVID & GUNNER.

AIN'T WHOLE WHEAT.

BERNICE.

DOUGH BOY FACE.
YOU GOT THE CUTEST LITTLE DOUGH BOY FACE.

CLARA.

GOTTA BE STRONG MAKE THE MUSCLES TOUGHEN,
GOTTA BUN IN THE OVEN AND IT AIN'T NO MUFFIN.

KANUTE & AARVID & GUNNER.

AIN'T NO MUFFIN.

BERNICE.

BABY BUMP, YOU'RE SO PLUMP,
JUST LIKE RISING FOCACCIA.

CLARA.

NO MORE KISSIN', NO MORE HUGGIN',
NO MORE SQUEEZIN', NO MORE LOVIN',
CAUSE I'M BAKIN' PUMPERNICKEL IN MY LADY OVEN.

KANUTE & AARVID & GUNNER.

LADY OVEN.

BERNICE.

HELLO MY CORN BREAD, HELLO MY FRUIT CAKE,

HELLO MY FARMHOUSE LOAF.

CLARA.

I GOT A FIRE DOWN BELOW BECAUSE THE BREAD IS DONE.

SOMEONE PUT SOME BUTTER ON MY HOT CROSS BUN.

KANUTE & AARVID & GUNNER.

HOT CROSS BUN.

BERNICE.

HUSH LITTLE CALZONE DON'T YOU CRY.

MOMMA HOPES YOU GRADUATE FROM JUNIOR HIGH.

CLARA.

I'M AT THE END OF THE ROAD AND I'VE COME FULL STOP.

I GOTTA BUN IN THE OVEN AND I'M READY TO POP.

BERNICE & KANUTE & AARVID & GUNNER.

READY TO POP.

(They all take out bobby pins and pop their balloons.)

CLARA.

WORD.

AARVID. *(to GUNNER)* Now, that wasn't so bad, was it?

GUNNER. No, it was actually kinda fun. *(He laughs, then quickly stops.)* Okay, now you're tryin' to cheer me up.

(The roof creaks and the lights flicker, but stay on.)

CLARA. *(feeling a sharp pain)* Ahh!

GUNNER. Look, if the roof comes down, it'll be gradual, okay. We'll all have time to get under the kitchen table.

KANUTE. Ya know, since we're probly all gonna die, maybe we should all write one of those things that they put in the obituaries.

BERNICE. Epitaph.

KANUTE. Gezundheit. *(proud of his joke)* Nailed it!

BERNICE. Hey, how about this, why don't we all say somethin' about ourselves that the others don't know.

KANUTE. Yah, kind of like a death bed confession.

BERNICE. Yah. I'll start. This is somethin' you might not know about me...I dated Sven Yorgensen.

KANUTE. So did Clara.

CLARA. *(to* **BERNICE***)* We should trade stories.

GUNNER. *(sarcastic)* Oh, goody, cause I love stories about the guys my wife dated before me.

AARVID. *(to* **BERNICE***)* You dated Sven Yorgensen?

BERNICE. Yah. It was just a couple times while we were playin' the Holiday Inn in Nova Scotia. Nothin' serious. I just, well, I wanted to tell ya cause I think trust is the most important part of a relationship, ya know. So, is there anything you'd like to tell me, Aarvid?

AARVID. *(thinks)* Okay, fine...I'm not Lutheran.

KANUTE. Holy cheesecakes.

BERNICE. You're not?

AARVID. No...I'm Catholic.

KANUTE. Game changer! *(to* **CLARA** *and* **GUNNER***)* He's a closet Catholic.

AARVID. I go to a Catholic Church in Hibbing.

KANUTE. He might as well just be a Scientolocist.

AARVID. Kanute was gonna tell ya anyway. *(to* **KANUTE***)* That was the secret ya had about me, right? "I know what ya do in Hibbing."

KANUTE. I don't know what ya do in Hibbing. I just said that to mess with ya.

AARVID. Dangit. *(to* **BERNICE***)* I'm sorry I lied. I just...I didn't wanna lose ya.

BERNICE. You won't lose me. I don't care if you're Catholic.

KANUTE. Seriously?!

BERNICE. Thank you for your honesty. It makes me love you even more.

KANUTE. Oh, jeez...Okay, well, in that case, I too would like to unburden myself with something.

GUNNER. Please don't.

KANUTE. When I was learning how to ride a bike–

GUNNER. Oh, he's goin' back to his childhood.

CLARA. No, this was last week.

KANUTE. I realized that life is short and ya have to follow your dreams, so…I got Aarvid fired from his job.

AARVID. That was you?!

BERNICE. You what?!

KANUTE. *(to BERNICE)* Well, when I knew you were comin' back I called his boss and told him Aarvid was stealin' from the company.

AARVID. You have reached a new low.

KANUTE. Hey, I'm just bein' honest. *(to BERNICE)* I figured if he didn't have a job, you wouldn't wanna go out with him…So, do ya love me even more, now?

BERNICE. Okay, "A," no, "B," you're gonna call Aarvid's boss and tell him the truth, and "C," you're gonna get Aarvid's job back. With a raise.

AARVID. *(to KANUTE)* "Nailed it."

CLARA. Gunner, is there anything you'd like to confess?

GUNNER. No?

CLARA. *(exasperated)* What was I even thinkin'?

BERNICE. About what?

CLARA. I can't raise a child with someone who can't love. *(to GUNNER, emotional)* I mean, it's one thing not to love me, but…our child? *(The roof creaks and the lights flicker. CLARA looks up.)* Oh, come on!

KANUTE. *(trying to calm CLARA)* Gunner, you're a lucky guy to have someone like Clara. *(to BERNICE and AARVID)* I mean, when I first met Clara, I thought Gunner was holdin' her against her will.

GUNNER. Yah, I know I'm outta my league, okay. Ya don't have to remind me, alright…Okay, you want a confession? Okay, here. I live in fear every day that Clara is gonna leave me. Uh huh. And when she finally has the baby, I'll be an afterthought.

CLARA. *(She looks at the others.)* I'm sorry, was that Gunner that just said that?

GUNNER. Oh, that's good. I finally say somethin' personal and ya poke fun at me.

CLARA. No, no, I'm sorry, I was just, ya know…taken off guard.

AARVID. *(to GUNNER)* Interesting. Your behavior is a defense mechanism for your own insecurity.

GUNNER. Really? Tell me less.

CLARA. *(feels a sharp pain)* Ahh! *(She looks at her watch. In pain:)* Five minutes. Keep talkin'.

BERNICE. *(reading the book)* It says it's typical for the father to be jealous of the child. Especially during breast feeding.

KANUTE. *(to CLARA, holding up the breast pump)* Got milk?

(He pumps it, making "pump" sounds.)

BERNICE. Do you have any boundaries at all?

KANUTE. I will not go to East Grand Forks.

AARVID. You're doin' great, Gunner.

GUNNER. Ya want another one? Okay, here ya go. I'm terrified that I'm gonna be a horrible father to my child, okay. I can't even say, *(He murmurs the words, barely audible.)* "I love you" to my wife.

AARVID. I'm proud of ya, Gunner. Ya made some progress today.

KANUTE. *(to GUNNER, holding a box of tissues)* Tissue?

(GUNNER shoots him a look. He puts the tissue down.)

CLARA. Since we're opening up, I think we should tell 'em the pet names we had for each other.

GUNNER. Absolutely not.

KANUTE. Are you kiddin', what were they?

GUNNER. Don't tell him. He'll just use it against me.

CLARA. I used to call him "Leech Lips." Cause when we kissed, he would–

GUNNER. Okay, okay, nobody wants to hear that.

BERNICE. Oh, I do.

KANUTE. So do I.

AARVID. So do I.

CLARA. And he would call me Sugar Buns, cause he would take powdered sugar, and–

GUNNER. Okay, this is outta control.

(The roof creaks and a wolf howls. The lights flicker but stay on.)

Where's that gun?!

(He goes into the bathroom.)

CLARA. What are ya gonna do?

AARVID. I vote for shootin' Kanute.

BERNICE. Second.

CLARA. No. Just wing him.

KANUTE. Do I get a say in this?

BERNICE. No.

GUNNER. *(coming out of the bathroom with the gun)* I'm gonna scare away the wolves.

(He puts his coat on.)

CLARA. No, don't go out there. They might get ya.

GUNNER. Someone's gotta do it.

KANUTE. Don't look at me.

GUNNER. Wish me luck.

(GUNNER goes out the door.)

CLARA. No, don't, oh, be careful! Oh, jeez. *(She feels a twinge of pain.)* Ah.

(CLARA and BERNICE look out the upstage window, KANUTE and AARVID look out the downstage window. Two gun shots ring out.)

BERNICE. The wolves are scattering.

KANUTE. *(Channeling Schwarzenegger in* Terminator II*)* They'll be back.

(We hear a huge thump.)

AARVID. What was that?

CLARA. Looks like the gun shots made the snow fall off the roof.

BERNICE. *(to* **CLARA**, *reassuring)* We're not gonna die! That's positive.

*(****GUNNER*** *comes in the front door covered in snow.)*

GUNNER. There was a snowvalanche.

KANUTE. I told ya!

AARVID. Good work, buddy!

CLARA. *(She groans in pain.)* Ahhh! *(She looks at her watch. In pain.)* Okay, that's...oh, gosh, oh, gosh, that's three minutes. It's happening. Release the Kraken!

GUNNER. *(taking off his coat, panicking)* What do we do?! What do we do?!

CLARA. *(in pain)* I'm gonna need drugs!

KANUTE. Take a couple shots of Tequila...That's what my mom did.

CLARA. I don't want a Kanute baby!

BERNICE. Get her on her back!

GUNNER. I'm not sure I'm ready for this!

CLARA. You got one minute to get ready!

*(****AARVID*** *and* ***KANUTE*** *lift her up and put her on the stage center table, legs spread out to the audience.)*

Not here! Not here! There.

(She waves her arm, motioning for them to take her in the kitchen. They think she's motioning to take her to the bar. They carry her to the bar.)

*(****GUNNER*** *starts to faint. He goes down to one knee.)*

KANUTE. Gunner's goin' down!

CLARA. Do not faint on me!

GUNNER. *(starting to get up)* I got it! I got it! I'm okay! No, I'm not! *(goes down to one knee again)*

*(****AARVID*** *and* ***KANUTE*** *try to put* ***CLARA*** *on top of the bar.)*

CLARA. Keep it together, Gunner! *(to* **AARVID** *and* **KANUTE**) Not here ya hosers! In the kitchen! On the table! It's clean!

(They carry her in the kitchen. BERNICE follows them in.)

GUNNER. I love you.

CLARA. Liar!

GUNNER. *(He gets up.)* Okay, I'm ready. *(He pulls it together.)* First, I gotta go to the bathroom–

(heads to the bathroom)

CLARA. *(offstage)* Get in here!–

GUNNER. *(making a quick about face)* Okay, we'll do that later, then.

(On the way to the kitchen, GUNNER faints.)

CLARA. *(offstage)* Where's Gunner?!

(AARVID and KANUTE come back into the bar from the kitchen to see GUNNER on the ground, out cold.)

AARVID. Gunner! Gunner!

CLARA *(offstage)* Where is he?!

KANUTE. He's down.

AARVID. He fainted. C'mon, Gunner, get up, buddy. You can do it. Clara needs ya.

CLARA. *(offstage)* Where's Gunner?!

(We hear the "ding, ding, ding" from the movie, "Rocky," when he's trying to get up in the ring at the end. Everything goes into slow motion as GUNNER tries to regain consciousness and get up off the floor. AARVID and KANUTE cheer GUNNER on in slow motion.)

KANUTE & AARVID.	CLARA. *(offstage)*
(in slow motion)	*(in slow motion)*
Come on, Gunner! You can do it! Get up! Clara is havin' a baby! *(Etc.)*	Gunner, where are you! I need you! Get in here! *(Etc.)*

(They keep cheering him on. Like in the original Rocky, GUNNER gets half way up, then falls down several times. He finally gets up on his feet and holds his arms up like Rocky. When his arms go up we hear the "Rocky" theme song.)

GUNNER. I'm comin', Clara!

    (**KANUTE** *holds up the book for* **GUNNER.**)

Don't need it. In your face, La-maze class!

    (*He hurries into the kitchen.*)

KANUTE. I'm freakin' out!

AARVID. Don't lose it, okay. Just relax.

    (*The music starts.*)

KANUTE. Easy for you to say. You've never had a baby in a bar.

AARVID. Neither have you.

KANUTE. I visualized it.

    (**CLARA** *cries out in pain, making* **KANUTE** *cry out.*)

Ahh!

AARVID. Just settle down, would ya?

KANUTE. I can't!

    SONG - "Relax The Nerves"

AARVID. (*sings*)

    CALMING FORCES HELP RELAX THE NERVES.

GUNNER. (*offstage*) Push!

    (**CLARA** *cries out in pain, making* **KANUTE** *cry out.*)

AARVID.

    NEED TO BE STRONG RIGHT NOW SHE DESERVES IT.

    (**CLARA** *cries out in pain.* **KANUTE** *cries out a little.*)

    TAKE A DEEP BREATH AND THEN YOU LET IT OUT.

GUNNER. (*offstage*) Push!

    (**CLARA** *cries out in pain.* **KANUTE** *cries a little.*)

AARVID.

    LOOSENS YOUR BODY THROUGHOUT.

CLARA. (*offstage*) I can't do it!

GUNNER. (*offstage*) Yes, you can! Push!

    (**CLARA** *cries out in pain.*)

KANUTE.

SOUNDS LIKE CLARA'S BACK IS BEING CANED.

(**CLARA** *cries out in pain.*)

I WILL HELP YOU, DON'T DESPAIR.

(**KANUTE** *runs into the kitchen with the camera, recording.*)

AARVID. (*watching him go into the kitchen*) Ah, Kanute.

GUNNER. (*offstage*) Push!

(**CLARA** *cries out in pain.*)

AARVID.

THINKING HAPPY THOUGHTS WILL CLEAR THE BRAIN.

CLARA. (*offstage*) Is that Kanute?!

AARVID.

OF WHAT'S HAPPENING IN THERE.

CLARA. (*offstage*) Get out!

KANUTE. (*coming out of the kitchen*)

WHY DID I GO IN THE KITCHEN, WHO KNOWS.

THOUGHT THAT SOMETHING WAS WRONG.

GUNNER. (*offstage*) Push!

(**CLARA** *cries out.*)

KANUTE.

THAT I COULD HELP HER ALONG.

HOLY CRAP WAS I WRONG.

CAN'T GET THAT IMAGE FROM MY BRAIN STEM.

HEAD ALL SLIMY, LOOKIN' JUST LIKE E.T.

BREAKIN' OUT IN A SWEAT.

GUNNER. (*offstage*) Push!

(**CLARA** *cries out.*)

KANUTE.

SOMETHING I'LL NEVER FORGET.

EVERYTHING WAS ALL WET.

(*He looks at the camera playback and winces.*)

GUNNER. (*offstage*) C'mon, honey, one more!

(**CLARA** *cries out in pain.*)

AARVID.

CHILD BIRTH IS OH SUCH A BEAUTIFUL THING.

KANUTE. *(looking at the camera, wincing)* No, it isn't.

AARVID.

HAVING A BABY, WHAT JOY IT WILL BRING.

KANUTE. *(looking at the camera)* There's no joy in there.

AARVID.

LAUGHING AND GIGGLING AND WATCHING THEM PLAY.

KANUTE. *(looking at the camera)* No one's laughing, either.

AARVID.

BABIES BRING HAPPINESS EACH DAY.

(We hear the baby crying. **BERNICE** *comes out of the kitchen.* **BERNICE, KANUTE** *and* **AARVID** *sing the final round at the same time.)*

KANUTE.	**BERNICE.**	**AARVID.**
WHY DID I GO IN THE KITCHEN, WHO KNOWS. THOUGHT THAT SOMETHING WAS WRONG. THAT I COULD HELP HER ALONG. HOLY CRAP WAS I WRONG. CAN'T GET THAT IMAGE FROM MY BRAIN STEM. HEAD ALL SLIMY, LOOKIN' JUST LIKE E.T. BREAKIN' OUT IN A SWEAT. SOMETHING I'LL NEVER FORGET. EVERYTHING WAS ALL WET.	CHILD BIRTH IS OH SUCH A BEAUTIFUL THING. HAVING A BABY, WHAT JOY IT WILL BRING. LAUGHING AND GIGGLING AND WATCHING THEM PLAY. BABIES BRING HAPPINESS EACH DAY.	CALMING FORCES HELP RELAX THE NERVES. NEED TO BE STRONG RIGHT NOW SHE DESERVES IT. TAKE A DEEP BREATH AND THEN YOU LET IT OUT. LOOSENS YOUR BODY THROUGHOUT.

BERNICE & **KANUTE** & **AARVID**.

    BABIES BRING HAPPINESS EACH DAY.

BERNICE. It's a girl.

KANUTE. *(to **AARVID**)* You owe me five bucks.

AARVID. Does it look like Kanute?

BERNICE. No, she's normal.

AARVID. *(to **KANUTE**)* We're even.

BERNICE. We need to celebrate. Let's break out the fancy
    stuff.

KANUTE. Beer mimosas!

    (He goes behind the bar.)

BERNICE. It came out real fast. It was like, "Get me outta
    here!" Gunner was awesome. He really came thru. He
    was like, "push, push," then I passed out–

AARVID. Wait, what?

BERNICE. Just for a minute. And when I came to, Gunner
    had delivered the baby.

KANUTE. *(coming back around the bar)* I got some video of it.

    *(He holds the camera in front of **AARVID** and **BERNICE**.)*

AARVID & **BERNICE**. *(Looking at the video. Cringing.)* Ohhh!

    (looking away)

KANUTE. *(looking at the video)* Ya know, as horrible as it is, I
    can't seem to take my eyes off it.

    *(**GUNNER** comes out of the kitchen holding the baby.)*

AARVID. Oh, look at that, there she is.

    *(**AARVID** and **KANUTE**, with video camera, go over to
    GUNNER and the baby.)*

BERNICE. Where's Clara?

GUNNER. Cleanin' up.

BERNICE. I'll go check on her.

    (She goes into the kitchen.)

AARVID. Congratulations, Gunner.

GUNNER. Thanks.

KANUTE. (*videoing* **GUNNER** *and the baby*) Yah, that's it, Gunner, support the head, hold it like a football. But don't spike it. (*looking at the baby*) Oh look, her eyes are just like yours except full of hope.

AARVID. I'm proud of ya, big guy. You got some big 'ol cojones, there.

GUNNER. Isn't she beautiful? Just like her mother.

AARVID. Yah, she's beautiful.

KANUTE. Can I keep the placenta for bear hunting?…It attracts bear, better than a cub scout.

GUNNER. Ignoring that.

KANUTE. So are ya gonna be okay, ya know, havin' a girl?

(*He grabs a fish scale off the bar wall.*)

GUNNER. Are you kiddin' me? I always wanted a girl.

KANUTE. Hey, let's weigh it. (*holding the fish scale toward* **GUNNER**)

GUNNER. Not with a fish scale.

AARVID. So, how does it feel to be a father?

(**GUNNER** *looks at* **AARVID**, *thinking, but not responding*)

KANUTE. (*videoing* **GUNNER**) Yah, how does it feel, Gunner?

(**GUNNER** *thinks but doesn't respond*)

Okay, let's use your out loud words.

(*The music starts.*)

SONG - "Words Can't Express"

GUNNER. (*sings*)
WORDS CAN'T EXPRESS THE EMOTIONS YOU FEEL
WHEN YOUR NEW BORN FIRST CRIES,
THEN OPENS HER EYES
AND SLOWLY LOOKS UP TO YOU.
A GIFT FROM ABOVE, OF INSTANT LOVE,
LOVE THAT IS PURE AND TRUE.

(**CLARA** *slowly walks out of the kitchen with* **BERNICE** *and sits, center table.*)

GUNNER. *(sings)*
>   I CAN'T DESCRIBE THESE FEELINGS INSIDE,
>   THE FEELINGS I ONE TIME KNEW.
>   ON THAT GREAT DAY, THAT PERFECT DAY.
>   THE DAY THAT I MARRIED YOU.

>   *(He hands the baby to* **CLARA**.*)*

>   ON THAT DAY I PROFESSED MY LOVE.
>   LOVE TILL DEATH DO US PART.
>   NOW YOU'VE GIVEN ME BRAND NEW LOVE,
>   CAPTURING MY HEART.

>   HOW CAN I THANK YOU FOR BRINGING
>   SUCH HAPPINESS INTO MY LIFE.
>   MY BEAUTIFUL WIFE.
>   YOU HOLD TO MY HEART THE KEY.
>   I KNOW THAT I SHOULD SAY IT MORE,
>   YOU MEAN THE WORLD TO ME.

>   I NEED TO SAY, I LOVE YOU TODAY.
>   MUCH MORE THAN THE DAY BEFORE.
>   IF YOU'LL BE MINE TILL THE END OF ALL TIME.
>   I VOW I'LL LOVE YOU FOREVER MORE.

>   *(***GUNNER*** goes down on one knee, and takes* **CLARA***'s hand.)*

>   IF YOU'LL BE MINE TILL THE END OF ALL TIME.
>   I VOW I'LL LOVE YOU FOREVER MORE.

>   *(The song ends. They kiss.)*

>   I love you, Clara.

CLARA. I love you, too, Gunner.

GUNNER. Will you marry me? Again?

CLARA. Yah, sure, you betcha.

>   *(They kiss.)*

BERNICE. I think I'm gonna cry.

KANUTE. I think I threw up in my mouth a little.

CLARA. Thank you for delivering our baby.

GUNNER. Yah, well, *you* were the real star in there. And we couldn'ta done it without Bernice.

CLARA. *(to* **BERNICE***)* Thank you so much.

BERNICE. Oh, you betcha. Sorry about the fainting part.

CLARA. Oh, no problem. *(to* **GUNNER***)* Are you cryin'?

GUNNER. What? No. I'm just…sweatin' outta my eyeballs.

CLARA. Okay.

GUNNER. I am truly, madly and deeply in love with you, Clara. I love you so much, I–

CLARA. Okay, Gunner, that's good. Any more and I'll think ya got possessed by aliens…Ya know, sayin' it once a week is just fine, okay. Even once a month.

GUNNER. Can I say it once a day?

CLARA. I don't have a problem with that.

(They kiss again.)

BERNICE. They're perfect together.

KANUTE. Like whiskey and hunting.

BERNICE. Yah.

KANUTE. *(putting the video camera down)* I just wanna say, I'm not really proud of some of the things I did back there. I mean, I know the stress of the whole snow storm got to all of us.

BERNICE. No. Pretty much just you.

KANUTE. I also wanna say, I wasn't a hero today.

AARVID. Not even close.

KANUTE. We were all heros.

BERNICE. Except you.

KANUTE. I just did what anyone else would do.

AARVID. Panic like a lost child at KMART.

KANUTE. Yup.

GUNNER. I never wanna lose ya, Clara. Ya mean the world to me.

CLARA. I'm not lettin' ya go, Gunner. Unless we're cousins, then we'll end up in separate jails…Oh, gosh, that reminds me… *(picking up the phone, putting it to her ear)* It's workin'. *(She dials the phone.)*

GUNNER. Who ya callin'?

(**KANUTE** *sings the* Deliverance *banjo song. To* **KANUTE.**)

Really? Again?

CLARA. *(phone to her ear)* Mom?…Yah, I just had the baby. In the bar…It's a girl…Yah…Gunner delivered it…Yah, he *is* good for somethin'. Listen, umm, it seems that Gunner and I are first cousins, and…Oh, you know?… Uh huh…Okay…Yah, thanks, Mom. I gotta go…I like you, too…Okay, bye.

(*She hangs up. Everyone is waiting to hear the result.*)

We are related.

GUNNER. Crap.

CLARA. But it's not a blood relationship.

GUNNER. Yes!

CLARA. I was adopted.

(*She smiles and looks at the baby.*)

KANUTE. Did she just say–

GUNNER. Three, two, one–

CLARA. *(looking straight ahead)* I was adopted!?

GUNNER. Baby first, honey. We'll deal with that later. One thing at a time.

(*He puts his arm around* **CLARA.**)

AARVID. *(to* **BERNICE**) So, I was thinkin' about the baby thing, and I'm kinda excited to have a baby–

BERNICE. I don't wanna have a baby right now.

AARVID. Wait, what?

BERNICE. Well, watchin' what Clara just went thru, I think I'd like to hold off on havin' a baby for, oh, I don't know, five or ten years.

AARVID. Really?

BERNICE. Yah, right now I think I'd rather be water boarded than go thru that.

AARVID. Well, are we still gettin' married?

BERNICE. Ya know, why don't we just kinda play that one by ear.

KANUTE. Still in the game!

BERNICE. But we can go out.

AARVID. Sweet!

(*BERNICE and AARVID hug.*)

KANUTE. Dangit.

(*A wolf howls. Channeling* Poltergeist.)

They're baaaaaack.

AARVID. (*looking out the window*) Hey, the snow stopped.

BERNICE. It's clearin' up.

GUNNER. Hey, there's a dog sled comin' up the path. Oh, hey, it looks like Ruth and Martha and Helen and...

CLARA. Who's drivin' it?

GUNNER. (*despondent*) Trigger...my sister.

AARVID. The wolves are scattering.

GUNNER. They must know her.

KANUTE. Before the reporters get here and wanna interview me, I wanted to give ya a little baby present.

CLARA. Is it a gun?

KANUTE. No.

(*He takes out a check and hands it to* GUNNER.)

Here.

(*GUNNER looks at the check.*)

GUNNER. Ten thousand dollars?...I can't accept this.

(*He holds it out to* KANUTE.)

CLARA. (*grabbing the check from* GUNNER) I can. (*to* KANUTE) What are your terms?

KANUTE. I wanna be the Godfather.

CLARA. (*She looks at* GUNNER, *then back to* KANUTE.) Supervised visits only. No advice to the child unless we approve it first. No more tellin' jokes. That one's for me. And if somethin' happens to me and Gunner, custody will go to the Godmother.

KANUTE. Who's that?

CLARA. Bernice.

>(**BERNICE** *gasps.*)

>If you'd like to be.

BERNICE. Oh, my gosh, yes. Oh, it's such an honor. Thank you.

CLARA. *(to* **KANUTE***)* If that happens, Kanute, you'll fully support our child financially. *(to* **GUNNER***)* You okay with this?

GUNNER. Yah, if you are.

CLARA. Congratulations, Godfather.

KANUTE. Awesome! Can I make a speech?

CLARA. No.

KANUTE. Okay.

AARVID. *(handing* **CLARA** *his present)* Here, open my present.

CLARA. *(She looks in the gift bag.)* Oh, thank you. What is it?

AARVID. A Lifestyle System, Baby Edition.

CLARA. Oh, how sweet.

AARVID. *(to* **KANUTE***)* Cause money can't buy love.

KANUTE. You haven't been to Duluth.

>*(The music starts.)*

>**SONG - *"Babies and Beer - Reprise"***

EVERYONE. *(singing)*
>PEANUTS AND PRETZELS AND BABIES AND BEER.
>THEY MAKE THE WORLD GO ROUND.
>HAVING A BEER WILL BRING JUBILANT CHEER,
>AND HELP YOU STAY UNWOUND.

>HAVING A BABY WILL MAKE LIFE COMPLETE.
>UNTIL THE COLLEGE YEARS.
>THEN YOU WILL WISH YOU HAD MILLIONS OF DOLLARS,
>BUT YOU DON'T, SO INSTEAD DRINK MORE BEERS.

>BABIES AND BEER.
>BABIES AND BEER.
>MAKE EVERYTHING ALRIGHT.
>PROBLEMS NO MORE, WITH EVERY POUR.
>YOU'LL SLEEP RIGHT THRU THE NIGHT.

(BERNICE and AARVID go behind the bar and get a baby bottle and three mugs of milk.)

RAISING A BREW,

HAPPY FOR YOU,

EMOTIONS RUNNING FREE.

BEST PART ABOUT YOU JUST MADE A BUDDY, A–

CLARA. *(interrupting everyone)*

MILK DRINKIN' BUDDY FOR ME.

(BERNICE hands her a baby bottle, and hands GUNNER a mug of milk.)

EVERYONE.

I'M SO DARN HAPPY YOU JUST MADE A BUDDY, A

MILK DRINKIN' BUDDY FOR ME.

(CLARA feeds the baby with the baby bottle, while GUNNER, AARVID and BERNICE raise their mugs of milk. KANUTE holds up the breast pump, squeezing it, making breast pump sounds.)

(blackout)

End of Play

PROPS AND COSTUME LIST

ACT I

Furniture:
  2 tables (30 – 36 inch diameter) (center stage, stage left)
  4 chairs without arm rests (right and left of each table)
  Bar (6-8 feet depending on size of set)
  2-3 bar stools

On Floor:
  Extremely large karaoke machine far stage left (see sample drawing)
  2 Karaoke song menus (on top of karaoke machine)
  Remote control for karaoke machine (on top of karaoke machine)

On Walls:
  Beer signs
  Stuffed fish and various other stuffed animals
  Coat hooks (by front door)

Behind bar:
  Liquor bottles
  Sports trophies
  Beer tower

Props and Dressing:
  On Tables:
    2 restaurant napkin holders with napkins - optional
    2 sets of salt and pepper shakers - optional
    4 food menus (2 on each table) - optional

On Bar:
  Deck of cards on bar dealt out for Gunner & Kanute's Gin game
  2 empty beer mugs for Gunner & Kanute
  Telephone - cordless
  Beef Jerky in a jar
  Radio
  Bowl of beer nuts
  Video camera

Under/Behind the Bar:
  "Pregnancy For Dummies" - Book
  Breast Pump
  2 Bar towels
  2 Beer mugs - 3/4 full of beer - for Gunner and Kanute
  Blown up balloons with tape on them (At least 5 - Bernice tapes
  them on the walls)
  Beer (for refills, preferably non-alcoholic)
  Yellow rubber kitchen gloves - Kanute wears them
  Measuring tape - Kanute uses it
  Cigar band - Clara gives it to Aarvid

Costumes:
  Pregnancy Belly for Clara
  Clara brings in:
    2 Brown paper bags with groceries
  Bernice brings in:
    Gift bag with baby shower present
  Aarvid brings in:
    Shoulder bag carrying gift bag with baby shower present
  Kanute carries with him:
    A ring box holding an engagement ring

ACT II

Under/Behind the Bar:
  Baby Bonnet and Baby Bib - Kanute puts them on at end of "Knee Deep" song
  Big Costume Baby Bottle - Kanute holds it up at end of "Knee Deep" song
  Fish Scale - Kanute uses it
  3 Mugs with Milk - Can make it look like mugs have milk in them with white paint inside mugs, or white paper lined mugs - for last "Babies and Beer reprise" song
  White real Baby Bottle - for last "Babies and Beer reprise" song

Hanging on back of chair, center stage table:
  Purse with lipstick in it - Gunner uses it in "Knee Deep" song

Costumes:
  Sexy dress for Bernice - wears it for "Little Miss Muffet" song (puts it on in the kitchen)
  Optional: Bernice could also wear sexy "Little Bo Peep" costume for the song

In the Kitchen:
  Bottle of Ketchup - Kanute brings it out
  Fake Baby wrapped in a blanket - Gunner brings it out
  Flannel shirt for Clara to put on after having the baby

In the Bathroom:
  Pistol (preferably fake) - Gunner brings it out
  Carving knives - Kanute brings them out
  Chef Hat - Kanute wears it
  Chef Apron - Kanute wears it
  Paper bag with holes cut out for eyes and mouth - Kanute wears it
  Plunger - Kanute brings it out
  Bag of Fava Beans - Kanute brings it out
  Bottle of Chianti - Kanute brings it out

Outside the front door:
  Fake snow flakes - Gunner has snow on shoulders when he comes back in

Optional:
- Rig it so the fake snow is in a trough, outside, above the window by the front door.
- Time the CD sound effect so Gunner is outside the window, ready to come back in, when the snow falls on him. Gunner can pull the rope on the trough, releasing the snow to fall on him.

COSTUMES

Other than the costume changes described above, the costumes for DON'T HUG ME, I'M PREGNANT reflect what people wear in a small rural northern Minnesota town in early October. That would include fall coats, jeans, corduroy, flannel shirts, sweaters, boots, and sturdy shoes. Aarvid would wear slightly nicer clothes, maybe a tie and khaki pants. Clara has a fake baby bump, so would wear a maternity top.

Sample Karaoke Design

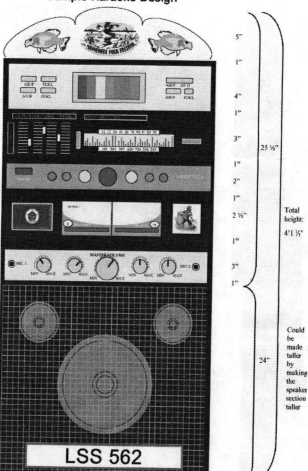

Lights
change
colors

Red lines

with
volume

Lights
blink on
and off

5"

1"

4"

1"

3"

1"

2"

1"

2 ½"

1"

3"

1"

25 ½"

Total
height:
4'1 ½"

24"

Could
be
made
taller
by
making
the
speaker
section
taller

LSS 562

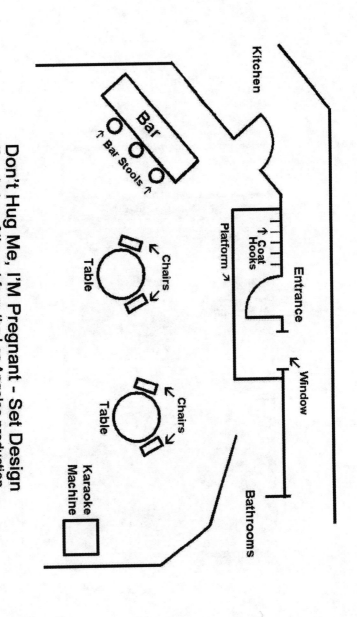

Don't Hug Me, I'M Pregnant - Set Design
(for photos of the set from the Los Angeles production,
visit: DontHugMe.com

Kitchen

Bar

↑ Bar Stools ↑

Platform

↑ Coat
Hooks

Entrance

Chairs

Table

Window

Chairs

Table

Karaoke
Machine

Bathrooms

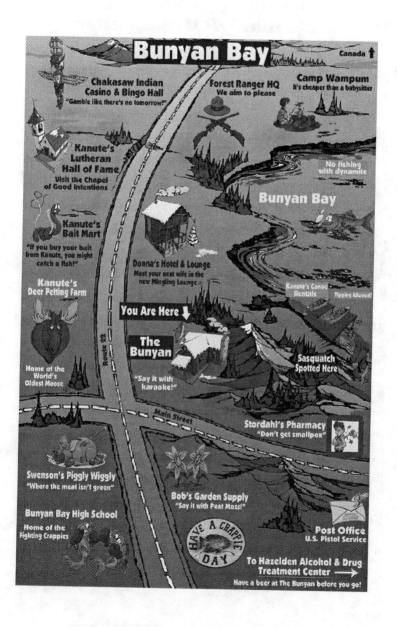

OTHER TITLES AVAILABLE FROM SAMUEL FRENCH

DON'T HUG ME

Book and Lyrics by Phil Olson
Music by Paul Olson

Musical Comedy / 3m, 2f / Interior

It's *Fargo* meets *The Music Man* (without the blood or the trombones).

Oh, for cryin' in yer snow shoes! It's the coldest day of the year in Bunyan Bay when a slick karaoke salesman arrives at the bar and turns the locals' lives upside down. With its over the top songs and crazy characters, this "Minnesota love story with singin' and stuff" will have you laughing until the spring thaw!

Don't Hug Me takes place in Bunyan Bay, Minnesota. Cantankerous bar owner, Gunner Johnson, wants to sell the business and move to Florida. Clara, his wife and former Winter Carnival Bunyan Queen, wants to stay. Bernice Lundstrom, the pretty waitress, wants to pursue a singing career. Her fiance, Kanute Gunderson, wants her to stay home. It's a battle of wills, and when a fast-talking salesman, Aarvid Gisselsen, promises to bring romance into their lives through the 'magic' of karaoke, all heck breaks loose!

Featuring the songs, "I'm a Walleye Woman in a Crappie Town," "My Smorgasbord of Love," and "I Wanna Go to the Mall of America."

"A hokey jokey karaoke crowd pleaser!"
– *Los Angeles Times*

"A lot of laughs!...A great time! Go see it!"
– Tom Barnard, KQRS

OTHER TITLES AVAILABLE FROM SAMUEL FRENCH

A DON'T HUG ME COUNTY FAIR

Book and Lyrics by Phil Olson
Music by Paul Olson

Musical Comedy / 3m, 2f / Interior

A Don't Hug Me County Fair is the summer sequel to the smash hit musical comedies *Don't Hug Me* and *A Don't Hug Me Christmas Carol!*

It's summer time and the Bunyan County Fair is approaching, the biggest thing that's happened in Bunyan Bay since the winter carnival snowplow parade. This year the Bunyan County Fair means one thing to Gunner and Clara Johnson, owners of a little bar called The Bunyan; The Miss Walleye Queen Competition. Bernice, the pretty waitress, sees this as her big chance to win Miss Walleye Queen, to be discovered, and more important, to have her face carved in butter at the Minnesota State Fair. The stakes have never been higher in Bunyan Bay. The trouble begins when Gunner's wife, Clara, decides she also wants to win Miss Walleye Queen. Bigger trouble arrives when Gunner's estranged twin sister, Trigger, (played by Gunner) shows up to try to win the beauty pageant.

Featuring 18 original songs including, "My Campfire is Burnin'," "I'm a Bunyan Woman," "If I Could Win Miss Walleye Queen," "Pontoon Ladies.", "I'm Just a Pretty Forest Ranger," and "Our Butter Face Queen."